Meet the Real World, Rachel

"Rachel, if you don't open this door and tell me what's going on now, I *am* going to go and get your mum!"

For a second there was silence, and then I heard a tiny *ftt!* sound. It was the sound of a bolt being drawn back. Before Rachel got a chance to change her mind, I barged in and shut the door behind me.

And there was Rachel, sitting on the lid of the loo seat, looking like the world had ended.

"Oh, Stella, you are going to think I'm a *complete* freak!"

Uh-oh.

What on earth was coming next? Was she going to admit to being a trainspotter or something? Or was she going to confess to being half-human, half-robot?

I dreaded to think. . .

KAREN McCOMBIE

meet the REAL WORLD, RACHEL

SCHOLASTIC

For Justine (my *Just 17* pal)

First published in the UK in 2004 by Scholastic Children's Books
An imprint of Scholastic Ltd
Euston House, 24 Eversholt Street
London, NW1 1DB, UK
Registered office: Westfield Road, Southam, Warwickshire, CV47 0RA
SCHOLASTIC and associated logos are trademarks and or registered trademarks
of Scholastic Inc.

This edition published by Scholastic Ltd, 2007

Text copyright © Karen McCombie, 2004
The right of Karen McCombie to be identified as the author of this work
has been asserted by her.

Cover illustration copyright © Spike Gerrell, 2004

10 digit ISBN 0 439 94293 4
13 digit ISBN 978 0439 94293 5

British Library Cataloguing-in-Publication Data
A CIP catalogue record for this book is available from the British Library

Printed by Bookmarque Ltd, Croydon, Surrey
Papers used by Scholastic Children's Books are made from wood grown in
sustainable forests.

1 3 5 7 9 10 8 6 4 2

www.scholastic.co.uk/zone

CONTENTS

From: *stella*
To: Frankie
Subject: Wish you were here! (Sniff!!)
Attachments: "Meet the real world, Rachel"

Hi Frankie!

Weird question, I know, but do you remember that time when me, you, and the others went to Camden Market and hung out on the little bridge over the lock? We were up for doing some boy-watching, weren't we, except that Lauren got in a right state when she saw a dead duck floating in the canal. Eleni tried to tell her that ducks don't drown, and Parminder said maybe it was just having a lie-down. But Lauren *still* stressed out, till the "duck" got nearer and Neisha pointed out that it was actually a kebab wrapper.

For some dumb reason, that memory of London and you guys *ping*ed into my head after the ambulance left the lido last week. Why, I don't know, since the whole lido thing was *properly* scary. I mean, Rachel definitely *wasn't* having a lie-down at the bottom of the pool that day, and she definitely *couldn't* have been mistaken for a kebab wrapper – not wearing that tiny, foxy bikini anyway!

Last time we spoke, you said it was amazing how obnoxious a girl could be, specially to people who'd just saved her life. Well, that's true, but it's a bit more complicated than that. So here's the whole saga as an attachment. Read it and see what you think of Rachel once you've checked it out. . .

OK, I'd better get off the computer – Jake and Jamie are hanging off each of my elbows, demanding to look at the Boohbahs website. (How tragically unglamorous is my life!)

Miss you ☹, but M8s 4eva ☺!

stella

PS Peaches brought me a present and left it on the bed for me this morning. Wow – how did my fat cat know that I'd *always* wanted a smelly insole for a size 42 trainer?

Juggle, juggle, *splat*

"*Ffffttttttffffffffffff...*"

Heatwaves and fur – they're not a great combination.

Peaches – flopped out on the desk in my den in the garden – made a sound like steam slowly hissing out of a leaky pipe.

Maybe all the hot air trapped in his furry body was escaping in that one feline sigh.

"Poor puss..." I muttered, wondering if I should put my paintbrush down and reach over to give him a sympathetic stroke – but that might make him even *hotter*.

Unless... unless I filled a rubber glove full of ice cubes and tried stroking him with *that*, of course!

Yep, the heatwave was melting my brain, if you hadn't noticed.

I decided I should just carry on with my painting and try to ignore the fact that I thought I might self-combust.

3

My painting seemed to distract Peaches too; his eyelids flipped open *just* wide enough for me to spy a glimmer of green and black. His pupils rapidly expanded and contracted as he focussed on the brush, which was daubing watercolours on the thick white paper only a few centimetres from his nose.

Peaches' whiskers twitched, and in a split-second, a hairy, fat paw extended, lazily trying to claw at the darting brush.

"Oi – don't spoil my picture!" I told him, moving the drawing pad closer to me.

Pretending he hadn't heard me, or done anything as silly and undignified as playing, Peaches sighed another sigh, curved his back into a reverse arch/stretch and gazed out of the tiny den window, towards the tent in the garden.

The tent that was bulging – and giggling.

"I bet you a tin of tuna that someone starts crying in the next two minutes," I muttered to Peaches.

The tent was my dad's idea of keeping my two-year-old brothers a) amused, and b) out of the sun. Dad had made a tiny clearing in our rainforest of a garden to put the tent up and then left Jake and Jamie to it, while him and Mum got on with some DIY in our wreck of a house.

So far – from the safety of my den – I'd seen

4

my twin brothers drag many (unexpected) things into the tent, including a box of cornflakes, their entire soft toy collection, both their tricycles, a potty, a tin of cat food, a wooden spoon, the clothes-peg bag, a plastic fireman's helmet, and my friend TJ's little sister Ellie.

TJ had dropped Ellie round here while he went to the house over the lane for a juggling lesson with the clowns who lived there.

Good grief. . .

Can you believe I just said that? Two weeks ago, I was living in a smart flat, in a trendy part of London, with a great room of my own and a bunch of very cool friends to hang out with.

Now I lived in a crumbly cottage in a snoozy seaside resort, hung out in a glorified garden shed, was best mates with a short lad with a big dog, and had *clowns* for neighbours.

At least one thing in my upside-down life hadn't changed. At least I still had my drawing and my painting – and even a sort of art studio to do it in, if you tried to forget that what I was sitting in used to be an ancient outside loo or laundry room once upon a time.

Boing.

That was one of my (zillions of) springs of hair, escaping from the scrunchie I'd bundled it into.

5

I'd also tried to keep my over-enthusiastic hair at bay on this meltingly hot Monday afternoon by clipping it back off my face with a mismatching collection of star, flower and fruit-shaped hair-grips.

Boing.

Great – another curl making its bid for freedom. Soon they'd all be sproinging and boinging in front of my face and I'd never be able to concentrate on the funky (i.e. not corny) fairy I was painting.

"Ahh-*wooooooo. . .!*" a hairy someone suddenly sighed.

Hey, what was I complaining about? In heatwaves like this, at least I could wear a vest-top and mini. Poor old Bob the dog was stuck with his thick, furry coat. It must be like wandering around with a duvet superglued to you. . .

Feeling sorry for him, I grabbed the old jam jar of water right beside me.

"Want some water?" I asked, glancing down at the hairy hunk of Alsatian panting on the cool-ish floor of my den.

"You can't give him that!" said a voice, as a (short-ish) figure blocked the sun in the doorway. "It's full of blue swirls . . . you've just scooshed your brush around in that, haven't you?"

TJ was right – I had indeed just scooshed, and swirls of Cerulean Blue were suspended in the H_2O that I'd nearly poured into the saucer by Bob's nose. I had no idea if Cerulean Blue watercolour paint was poisonous or not, but I liked TJ's dog a LOT, and the last thing I wanted to do was kill him. (It wouldn't look too good this early on in mine and TJ's friendship, I didn't suppose. It would be the equivalent of him losing one of my brothers on a stroll or something.)

"How did the juggling lesson go?" I asked TJ, plonking the blue water jar back on the table, while Bob gave a disappointed "humfff!" as the promised liquid didn't materialize.

"Brilliant!" grinned TJ, sticking his hands deep in his baggy skater trousers and pulling out an apple, a plum and a raggedy tennis ball. "Watch!"

As he started juggling, I frowned.

"They taught you to juggle *that* stuff?!" I asked, confused.

Mr and Mrs Mystic Marzipan (not their real names, if you hadn't guessed) were professional jugglers, as well as acrobats, puppeteers and clowns. I didn't think they'd normally recommend that people juggle with the leftovers of the fruit bowl and a tennis ball that looked like it had been chewed and spat out.

"Nah – I learned using some beanbag things of theirs. This ball is Bob's toy," panted TJ, trying to concentrate on the whirling three items he was chucking from hand to hand. "The other stuff . . . I sort of helped myself to from your kitchen table just now."

Aha . . . so it *was* from the fruit bowl. *Our* fruit bowl. Which made us sound like a very healthy family. Just as well no one could see that half a bag of cement and some weird plumbing gubbins were laid out alongside it on the kitchen table cum workbench.

"Did you notice that Ellie's being held hostage in the tent?" I asked, getting back to my fairy and deciding to paint her wings translucent pink.

"Uh-huh. Bossing two little boys about . . . bet she's loving it," said TJ, keeping up with his keepy-up.

"Hmm. . . I wouldn't bet on it *lasting* though. My brothers might be a few years younger than Ellie, but they're only going to behave for *so* long before they've got her covered in clothes pegs and are forcing her to eat cat food off a wooden spoon."

"Whatever. At least it gives me a break."

It might not have sounded like it, but TJ was actually pretty fond of his five-year-old sister.

8

What he *wasn't* so fond of was the fact that his mum expected him to be Ellie's more-or-less full-time babysitter/playmate/bodyguard for the holidays, and when you're a thirteen-year-old lad, that's just not exactly cool, is it?

"So what're you up to?" TJ asked, not taking his eyes off his whirling fruit and ball.

"Building a full-size replica of the spaceship from *Star Wars* out of dental floss," I mumbled, concentrating hard on not going over the lines with my paintbrush.

"Hey, see your fairy paintings?" TJ chatted on, *obviously* aware of what I was doing (so why did he ask?!) and *obviously* ignoring my sarky comment.

"Yep, I see them," I said, my eyes fixed on the nearly finished one in front of me. "What about them?"

"Well, they remind me of this film my mum forced me to watch once, 'cause she was starring in it."

"What film?" I asked, stopping what I was doing and turning to face the frantically juggling TJ.

From what he'd told me before about his mum (who I'd met a couple of times and didn't like much), she was one of these people who *say* they're actors but don't actually seem to *do* much acting.

"It was this thing set in the olden days. Like medieval times or something. It was about these two schoolgirls who saw fairies at the bottom of their garden and took photos of them."

"TJ, they didn't *have* cameras in medieval times!"

"Whatever."

I spotted a hint of a grin on TJ's face – and realized I was being wound up, in revenge for my dollop of sarkiness probably.

"So what star part did your mum have in this film anyway?" I asked him, ignoring the wind-up now I'd spotted it.

"A villager in the background, sort of milling about. She was on screen for about three whole seconds."

TJ wasn't especially close to his mum. I think she'd probably be better at *acting* the part of a mum, rather than really being one. It wasn't like she was cruel or horrible to him or anything, it's just that you got the feeling she'd rather be a hotshot big star in swanky West End theatres than be stuck in Portbay with two kids.

"Anyway, for a film about fairies it was pretty good," TJ continued, "'cause it was based on a true story."

"You mean, the girls *really* found fairies at the bottom of their garden?" I frowned, quickly glancing at the tangle of weeds, wildflowers and wilderness directly outside the window.

"No, Jamie!" Ellie's voice suddenly wailed. "*Don't* pull that out too or the whole tent will—"

"WHAAAAAA!"

I stood up quickly, to see what kind of disaster had struck in the garden, and saw Jamie hovering beside the remains of the tent. He was hugging a fluffy green crocodile who happened to be wearing a cornflakes packet at a jaunty angle on its head.

In Jamie's hand was a bundle of tent pegs freshly pulled from the ground. He looked very happy watching as Ellie – in a fireman's hat – dived back into the collapsed tent to rescue the wailing, Jake-sized lump from inside.

"Er. . ."

Now I turned back to see what the "er. . ." was about.

"Sorry, Stella – Jake shouting like that sort of made me *jump*."

Yeah, well, jumping was one thing; dropping the fruit and ball you were juggling was another, specially when an overripe plum had splatted against my jam jar and sent the blue-swirly water spilling all over my funky fairy.

I lunged forward, hoping I could maybe throw a wodge of tissues on to the picture before the mini-tidal wave did much damage. But I hadn't reckoned on Peaches swishing his huge, hairy tail across the whole sheet of paper, smudging the colours together even more.

"Apple?" asked TJ, holding out a peace-offering piece of fruit and looking like he was worried I might take it and bounce it off his head.

"You'd better think of something to cheer me up in the next five seconds," I told him sternly, before grabbing the apple and biting hard into it. (Mmm! The light dusting of cement powder added an interesting texture and taste. . .)

"I know the *exact* thing to cheer you up," TJ promised, as he tried to restrain Bob from lapping up a blue-ish puddle from the floor of the den.

"As long as it doesn't involve water, I'm happy," I said, rolling up my ruined, dripping artwork and sticking it in the bin.

TJ started choking.

Was it something I said. . .?

CHAPTER 2

Bad vibes and bellyflops

"Can you read it?" asked TJ, holding my phone in one hand and using the other as a five-fingered umbrella, keeping the screen in enough shadow for me to see the words that had just been texted to me.

"Yeah, thanks," I nodded, as I leant my elbows up on to the side of the pool.

Hi Stell – what u up 2? Love F

The message was from my best friend Frankie, back in London. The answer to her question – which I couldn't exactly text back since my fingers were wet – was that I was currently sploshing around and generally cooling off in Portbay's lido, along with half the town, it seemed.

It had been TJ's idea to come here, right after he'd juggled the contents of the jam jar of water over my painting this morning. And it was a brilliant idea, even if it *did* involve water, *and* big crowds. An outdoor pool, views of the sky while you're floating on your back, grass to lay your towel on and sunbathe, a vending machine selling ice-cold drinks . . . it was a pretty great way to spend a Monday afternoon.

"Do you want me to text Frankie back for you?"

"No, it's OK. Just shove my phone back in my bag for me, will you?" I asked TJ, feeling a tiny bit embarrassed about how much he was doing for me.

For a start, he'd suggested coming here. Then he'd bought me a Coke while I laid out my towel. Just now he'd wrestled my beeping phone out of my bag, called out to me in the pool, and bent down on his haunches, letting me read my text. I knew he was trying to make up for drowning my funky fairy, but all this attention made me feel like I had my own personal assistant. The thing was, I didn't want a PA – I wanted a friend.

"Why don't you come in the pool, TJ?" I asked him, as I bobbed around in the water, feeling the waves slap around me from the other splashing, shouting swimmers.

"Nah," he said, shaking his floppy head of fair hair and stuffing my phone back in the front pocket of my bag. "I've got that thing I want to read. And I've got to keep an eye on Ellie."

Ignoring the vintage *Superman* comic he'd brought with him, TJ walked barefoot back towards me and settled himself by the side of the pool, legs crossed, scrawny arms behind him, holding his weight.

OK, so I hadn't known him that long, but TJ still confused me sometimes. Just when I thought I'd got a handle on him (funny, sharp, with a bit of a chip on his shoulder about his height, or lack of it), he'd say or do something that threw me.

Like today – why suggest coming to hang out at a pool, and then sit overdressed in your jeans and T-shirt, while everyone around you's in shorts and bikinis?

And the thing about watching Ellie – *that* was an excuse too... She was five years old and fooling around with a bunch of kids in the toddler pool, paddling in about ten centimetres of water. She didn't need her big brother keeping an eye on her, and even if she did, he could do that from the main pool, wearing a pair of swimming trunks and having fun with me.

Anyone would think he was scared of the water, like he couldn't swim or something...

Ahh! Right – so maybe that's what this is about, I realized, as I scrunched my eyes against the dazzle of the sun and stared up at him. Fair enough; I wouldn't tease him. I'd learned my lesson when it came to teasing TJ about stuff he had a problem with. Last week, when I'd accidentally-on-purpose let slip about his real name in front of the horrible lads he'd been mucking around with, he'd looked at me like one of those poor, beaten-up, mistreated dogs in the leaflets for the RSPCA. (Never mind the Royal Society for the Prevention of Cruelty to Animals; I was half-tempted to report TJ's parents to the National Society for the Prevention of Cruelty to Children, for giving my friend the first name "Titus" and the middle name "J". And Ellie didn't get off lightly either; her full name is Electra Z. . .)

"Did you spot that Sam's gang are here?" said TJ, nodding his head somewhere to the right.

My heart instantly did a quick impression of a popcorn machine. How spooky that I was just thinking about them, and they turn out to be here. I didn't *dare* turn and make eye contact with them. After all, it was only yesterday that we saw them being caught by the police for vandalizing the old house round at Sugar Bay.

TJ would have been nabbed right along with

them – since Sam's lot were entertaining themselves by bullying him in between smashing things – if *I* hadn't turned up. Call it lucky, or call it embarrassing (it was both), but Sam's gang decided I must be TJ's girlfriend and laughed us both out of the place.

"What are they doing?" I asked TJ in a panic. "Are they looking over?!"

"Nah – they're standing round the side of the changing rooms, smoking and trying to look tough in front of the mums and toddlers," said TJ, grinning.

"But . . . but aren't you worried they're going to come over and say something?"

"Like what?" TJ shrugged. "Like tell us they got caught and cautioned by the police after we left them? No *way* – that would blow their cool. They think we were *long* gone, that we never saw a thing, and I guess that's the safest way to leave it."

I felt my cheeks flush pink as another memory from yesterday slithered into my mind. Me and TJ hunkered down in the sand at Sugar Bay, panicking that the police might spot us and think we were a splinter group of Sam's gang. So what did we do? The first thing we could think of, i.e. pretend we were a loved-up boyfriend and girlfriend, unaware of the crash-bang-walloping vandalism going on in the old house.

Before I went scarlet at the thought of our (eek!) emergency kiss, I bobbed my head under the water, letting the coolness calm my cheeks.

And for those couple of seconds that I held my breath and blinked at the pool tiles and the spangles of aqua and blue, yet *another* memory swam into my head. One from only half an hour ago, when I was waiting outside the lido for TJ and Ellie (who'd nipped home for Ellie's frilly swimsuit and to drop off a disgruntled Bob). There I was, standing daydreaming, wondering what all my old friends back in London were up to, when I'd found myself in a swirl of familiar sweet scents.

"Hello, dear!"

A-ha. . . Mrs Sticky Toffee. I really *would* have to ask her her real name sometime, but she tended to sneak up on me so suddenly – in an amazingly speedy way for an old lady – that she caught me out, every single time. Plus the toffees she was always trying to force on me; they kind of welded your teeth together, which made it hard to ask questions at the best of times.

"So where are you off to this afternoon, dear?" she'd smiled, opening her tiny, shiny cream handbag and pulling out a family-sized bag of toffees.

"Er, the lido," I'd replied, pointing to the sign directly above my head with one hand, and helping myself to a toffee with the other (well, it would be rude *not* to, wouldn't it?).

"The lido, hmm?" Mrs S-T frowned, adjusting her frothy pink netting hat. How she could bear to wear a hat and that apple-green raincoat of hers on such a meltingly hot day like today, I'd *no* idea.

"I haven't been here before. My friend TJ suggested it," I mumbled, before the chewed toffee started sticking like superglue.

"Well . . . you two be careful, now!" said Mrs S-T, nodding her head earnestly at me.

With that strange pronouncement, she stuffed her toffees back in her bag, snapped it shut and waddled off with a wave in place of a "bye".

I'd had a few encounters with Mrs S-T since my family had moved here to Portbay, and every single time, she'd managed to leave my mind completely frazzled. Why had she frowned at the mention of the lido? And what were me and TJ meant to be careful of? Sunburn? Well, *maybe*. . . I mean, there were plenty of prawn-pink holidaymakers wandering the streets of

Portbay at the moment, searching for ice creams to cool them down or pharmacists to sell them calamine lotion to pour on their badly toasted bodies.

Fffwhooosh!!!

With a rush and a splosh, my head was back above water, ready to face TJ again.

Only he wasn't alone.

"Hey. . . TJ says your name's Ella?"

The voice was high and girlish – if I'd had my eyes closed, I might have thought it belonged to someone not much older than Ellie.

But my eyes were as wide open as chlorinated water and bright sunlight would allow, and I saw that I was being spoken to (squeaked at?) by a skinny, pretty, dark-haired teenage girl, wearing the tiniest denim-look bikini. Behind her were three girls who were almost as pretty, but not quite, wearing almost as tiny bikinis, but not quite.

"It's Stella," me and an uncomfortable looking TJ corrected her at exactly the same time.

In a town where I only knew TJ, his sister, Peaches the cat, Bob the dog, an old lady who smelled of toffee and a bunch of thuggish lads who I didn't *want* to know, it would have been fun to be introduced to new people. And I wouldn't have minded the girl getting my name wrong, *usually*. (Well, we've all done it, haven't we? After all, I thought TJ was called Deejay at first.)

The only thing – OK, make that *things* – that put me off were. . .

a) None of the pretty girls were bothering to smile.

b) I had a feeling the girl had *deliberately* got my name wrong, just to put me in my place or something.

c) I recognized them all – they were the too-cool gang of girls that had been checking me out for the last couple of weeks around town.

"Stella. . . Ella. . . Whatever. . ." the dark-haired girl laughed, like I was boring her with details.

Rachel – *that*'s what her name was. TJ had told me *all* their names, but I recognized Rachel more than the others 'cause I'd also seen her on her own, coming out of her mum's arty-crafty gift shop, down on the prom.

But what suddenly struck me was the way she'd said my name; with the faintest hint of a lisp, like the "S" didn't quite want to roll off her tongue. What was *that* about? Was she putting it on, like the cutesy, girlie voice?

"It's Stella, not '*whatever*'," TJ frowned, staring up at her.

Rachel shrugged carelessly; her mates just sniggered at him.

The mates . . . what were their names again? Oh, yeah – Brooke, Hazel and Kayleigh – but I couldn't figure out which one of the staring, unsmiling girls was which.

"TJ says you've come from London," said one of the Brooke/Hazel/Kayleigh lot. The way she said "London", it was like she'd said "toilet".

For a second it looked like TJ was all set to answer again, but I didn't want him to. Back in London, I hid behind Frankie and Eleni and the others, letting them do my talking for me. But since I'd been in Portbay, I'd decided I didn't want to be shy-girl Stella any more. So I took a deep breath, vowed not to stammer, and spoke really fast.

"Yes – I lived in Kentish Town, really close to Camden Market. Do you know Camden Market? It's where lots of famous people go shopping, and it's where the MTV studios are."

Treading water, I blinked up at the crowd of girls, waiting for some kind of response. But the only kind of response I got was them all sneaking sideways looks at each other and sniggering, like I'd just said "I smell of wee".

I was thinking about slipping under water and

swimming away – as an alternative to wishing the ground would open up and swallow me – when another of the Brooke/Hazel/Kayleighs knelt down and lifted her sunglasses off her prettily piggish nose (all the better to stare at me).

"Hey, Ell— I mean, Stella," she said with a smirk. "Can we ask you something?"

"Uh-huh. . ." I nodded warily, wondering what was coming next. I was pretty sure it wasn't going to be an invitation to share an ice cream at the Shingles café with them later. . .

"How come," began the girl with the sunspecs, a hint of a grin playing on her glossed lips, "you look so sort of . . . permanently *tanned*?"

I felt my golden-brown skin pink up again. I *knew* what she was trying to say, in her clumsy, sarky way. And if she hadn't had that nasty grin on her face, like I was just some big, novelty joke to them, I'd have happily and proudly told them that three of my grandparents were white, but my grandad on my mum's side was black and that his family came from Barbados. And *that*'s why I didn't have milk-coloured skin like theirs. But with this lot, *however* I tried to explain my family background, it was going to come out sounding like I was apologizing for it, which was the *last* thing I'd want to do.

God, I suddenly really, *really* missed my friends and my old school. So Frankie and Neisha were black, and Parminder was Asian, and Eleni was Greek and Lauren's family were Irish, but all of us together were British and all of us together were just *us*, like everyone at my old school. Yeah, so you thought someone was nice or mean, kooky or boring, cute-looking or average, a sweetie or a nutter, but that was all about personalities, not about the colour of their skin, or whether their family came from Croydon or Mumbai or the *moon* or whatever.

"I. . . I. . ." I started to explain (OK, *stammer*), feeling my arms flail under the water and my words fail in my mouth as I struggled to say it the right way.

I saw Brooke, Hazel and Kayleigh (whichever one was which, whichever one was a witch) all eyeball each other and start giggling. Instinctively I switched my gaze to TJ for help . . . but he wasn't looking at me, he was staring up at Rachel, at the gorgeousness of Rachel probably. What boy could resist anyone so –

– oh.

Uh-oh!

I saw it all in a split-second; the weird fluttering of Rachel's eyes – like a slo-mo film speeded up too fast – and then the crumbling, as her whole body snaked downwards.

And then the splash, bigger than you'd think for someone so skinny, as she crashed into the water to the right of me. I don't know when exactly it sank into my head that she was in trouble; all I remember is seeing the horrified – almost weirdly *disgusted* – looks on Rachel's cronies' faces as she bellyflopped into the water. After that, some kind of auto-pilot kicked in, and I was under the water, heading through the spangles of blue and aqua towards Rachel, as she spiralled star-shaped towards the bottom of the pool.

Diving my way down towards her, the strangest thing happened; frantic darts and sparkles of bright light – lots of them – mimicked the spiral Rachel had just taken. Maybe it was just the sunlight refracting through the swirled pool-water, or maybe it was just some adrenaline rush sending pinpricks of brightness to my pupils, but for a second, it almost felt like there was *something* in the water, leading me to her. But what kind of something?

Fairies? Water sprites? I thought madly, as the pressure of holding my breath started to burn in my chest.

But all crazy thoughts of fairy magic disappeared as soon as I tried to get my arms under Rachel and lift her. Skinny as she was, her dead weight felt too much for me, specially since my lungs were struggling and pulsing for air.

Air and lightness, sun and breeze . . . it was exactly what I was craving as I struggled to get a hold of Rachel and propel her upwards. And then suddenly there was TJ, looking almost like a caricature of himself as the movement of the water played its tricks. Still in his jeans and T-shirt, TJ swam steadily down to Rachel's right side, grabbed her arm, and we were instantly moving upwards, the three of us heading towards the glittering sunlight as a pair of strong arms beckoned us up towards them. . .

Fffwhooosh!!!

For the second time in a few minutes, my head broke water.

"OK – I've got you!" a deep male voice said, as Rachel became weightless and disappeared out of my grasp.

It took my fuzzy head a moment or three to figure out that the lifeguard had now lifted Rachel safely out of the pool and was quickly checking her over.

And then it was my turn to be lifted out of the

pool, by two women who then threw a huge, lurid beach towel around my shoulders. They were some kids' mums – their freaked but excited children were staring at me like I was an alien.

They *stopped* staring at me as soon as the whirl of flashing ambulance lights veered into view and several people in uniform came scurrying across the grass, sending stunned sunbathers and swimmers swarming out of their way.

"Are you all right, miss?" an ambulance girl asked me, as her colleagues all huddled around Rachel's weirdly jerking body. (At least she was moving, at least that meant she was alive.)

"Uh-huh," I nodded frantically. "Is Rachel. . ."

"Don't worry, she's going to get all the help she needs," said the girl's calming voice, as she held my wrist and checked my pulse.

"And – and TJ? Where's TJ?" I asked in a panic, staring around me at the throng of whoever.

"I'm here. . ."

And so he was, just a couple of steps away from me, looking like a drowned rat, with his jeans and T-shirt and floppy hair soaking and sucked in tight to his body. Also sucked in tight to his body was Ellie, her small arms cuddling her brother in a steely, protective grip.

It was probably the stress and the tiredness, but

just for a second I thought again of those non-existent underwater fairies guiding me down towards Rachel. . .

Rachel.

Rachel nearly drowning.

Was *that* the something that spooky Mrs S-T had warned me and TJ to watch out for?

Honestly, I must have had a head full of chlorinated water to think anything as mad as that.

Mustn't I. . .?

CHAPTER 3

Splasharama

With the phone tucked under my chin, I used both hands to wring the water out of the front of my sopping wet T-shirt.

"Well, Stella my little star . . . you certainly had yourself quite a day, huh?" said Auntie V (for Vanessa), from the comfort of her arty, trendy flat in London.

"Yep, you could say that!" I replied, as I stood dripping in the bare, dusty living room of our ramshackle cottage.

The quite-a-day-thing: I'd just told Auntie V about this afternoon's excitement at the lido, where I'd felt like I was in an episode of *Casualty* or *ER* or something.

The dripping thing: I wasn't still wet from my life-saving escapade; I'd been helping Dad bathe the twins just now, right before Mum called me to the phone. (A wetsuit is really the ideal outfit when it's Jake and Jamie's splasharama.)

The bare-dusty-living-room thing: Dad had emptied the place and stripped out the old carpet, ready to re-plaster the walls tomorrow. And because there was nothing in the room apart from the phone, I'd thought I might as well wring the bath water out of the front of my T-shirt straight on to the floorboards.

"Weren't you scared when you dived down after that Rachel girl?" Auntie V asked me. "Or did it all just happen in a split-second?"

Now that I knew Rachel was OK (Mum had phoned the hospital when I got home), I could think about the whole thing more clearly. For about an hour after me and TJ had dragged Rachel out of the pool, my mind was just a messed-up jumble of images and thoughts, bouncing around in no order and making no sense ("Shock does that to you," Dad told me this afternoon, giving me a big hug).

The jumble in my head; it was all stuff like the sight of the intense flashing lights of the ambulance, TJ standing – shivering and skinny, Rachel's friends' blank faces ("They were probably in shock too, Stella," Dad had said), and even mad memories of hanging out at the canal back in Camden with Frankie and my old friends. And then, of course, there were all those glittery spangles of light in the water. . .

"I wasn't exactly scared," I say, plonking myself down on the floorboards and touching the mini puddle of water on the floor with my fingertips. "But it wasn't like a split-second thing either. It was more like. . ."

With one finger now tracing watery swirls through the dust, I hesitated, wondering if I should tell Auntie V what I hadn't mentioned to my parents.

"Like what, darling?"

Well . . . why not. If Auntie V ended up thinking I was mad as a fish, at least I wouldn't be able to see her disbelieving face, would I?

"Like I was somehow being led down to her. . ."

There was silence at the end of the phone. Uh-oh, she thought I was mad as a fish already, and I hadn't even *mentioned* the fairies.

Still, in for a penny, in for a pound, as Frankie's mum – always keen on her sayings – would, er, say.

". . .by fairies," I blurted out, feeling like I might as well finish the sentence, however nuts it sounded. "Well, these tiny, weaving dots of light in the water. They were sort of . . . *swivelling* down after her. Crazy, isn't it! Ha!"

I made out like it was just some dumb notion before Auntie V got the chance to tell me so herself.

"Hey, people see the strangest things in moments of crisis," said Auntie V, her voice sounding convincingly sincere. "I've read lots of articles about people seeing angels and all sorts!"

She was probably just trying to be nice. If someone told *me* they thought they'd seen an angel, I'd think they were mad as a *trawler* full of fish.

"Well, I guess it was just 'cause I had fairies on the brain today," I said, flopping myself back down on to the floor and staring up at the stained, desperately-in-need-of-a-lick-of-Dulux ceiling. "I was painting a ninja fairy this morning—"

"A *ninja* fairy?"

"They're my own invention," I explained, as my chest was gently crushed by Peaches meandering in and settling himself directly above my lungs in a purring, clawing, contented lump. "They're a cross between traditional, pretty fairies and Japanese animation."

"Oh, right," said Auntie V, though I suspected she didn't know what I was on about but was too polite to ask.

"Anyway," I continued, hoping I didn't sound

like I had asthma or whatever, since it was kind of hard to talk and breathe at the same time with the mighty weight of Peaches lying on me, "I was painting a ninja fairy this morning, and then TJ started talking about this film his mum was in. It was about a couple of girls in the early 1900s who photographed fairies at the bottom of their garden."

"Oh, yes – I know that story! And the photos turned out to be fake, didn't they?" Auntie V jumped in excitedly.

"Did they?"

What did I mean, "did they?" Why was I so surprised to hear that fairies didn't exist? (*Duh. . .*)

"Oh, yes! In the real story at least," Auntie V continued, in her confident, theatrical voice. "The photos were printed in the newspapers of the day and it was a sensation, because everyone thought they were genuine at first. I'm pretty sure that's the gist of it anyway."

"But how did they do it?"

I was confused. It wasn't like there were computers and Photoshop and CGI graphics kicking around in those days.

"Well, I think the girls just cut out these ethereal pictures of fairies, and then dotted them around a garden before photographing them. Or did someone do a clever trick and add the fairies in at the developing stage? I can't remember. But I do know the film you mean, Stella, because one of my clients was in it, as a soldier, or a postman or something, if I remember rightly!"

Auntie V works as an actors' agent. She gets them work in all sorts of areas, from tap-dancing musicals to ads for toilet roll.

"Yeah?" I croaked in surprise, as much as I could with a fat cat happily squashing the air out of my lungs.

"Oops . . . listen, Stella, darling, I don't want to cut you off, but I've got a call beeping through, and it's probably my client who's out working on a film about the Crusades in Morocco. He's in a terrible state about the camels on set spitting on him, and he's getting his chainmail knickers in a twist over the fact that the director isn't taking his complaints about the health and safety risks seriously. . ."

As Auntie V hurried off the line, I said my byes and hung up . . . and let my mind wander on to strange spangles again.

"Do *you* think they were fairies?" I mumbled to Peaches.

He answered with a steady prrrrr and a slow,

knowing blink of his heavy-lidded green eyes, which *could* have meant "Absolutely!", or maybe just meant he was very comfy, thank you.

Then it occurred to me that I should phone TJ and see how he was doing. He might not have been as fruitcakey as me and imagined seeing fairies, but after the whole Rachel scare, he'd looked sort of *spaced*.

Mind you, *I'd* been kind of spaced when something had dawned on me as I'd stood looking at my drowned rat of a mate. It obviously wasn't his lack of swimming skills that had kept TJ from stripping off and getting in the pool this afternoon (his help saving Rachel was proof of that). It was all about his size, again, wasn't it? In front of everyone at the Portbay lido, TJ didn't want to peel off his baggy skater jeans and T-shirt, and show them the skinny little dude that he was.

Poor TJ. . .

But as I listened to his mobile ringing, I suddenly got the giggles, as the vision of fairies in flippers and aqualungs swam into my soggy brain.

Me laughing must have been the equivalent of a bucking bronco ride for Peaches. His forehead instantly went into a feline frown, and he dug his claws into my T-shirt (and the skin under it), clinging on *hard*.

"Hello?"

"*Yeeeeeooooooooow!*"

"Who's this?" TJ's voice asked in confusion.

"Sorry – *eek*!" I gasped, trying to extricate ten pin-sharp claws from my chest. "It's me, Stella!"

"Stella? What's up? You sound weird!"

"I'm OK – I've just got a cat stapled to my chest, that's all. How're *you* doing?"

For a second, there was no reply . . . just a panting noise, which I suspected was Bob, rather than TJ.

"Pretty freaked, really," my friend answered (the panting carried on as he spoke, so I knew I'd guessed right and Bob was the phantom panter). "I mean, I don't particularly *like* Rachel, but I keep thinking, what if she'd drowned? And how come she fainted or whatever in the first place?"

I could have told him that there was no point thinking depressing stuff like that, and that she was in hospital, which was the best place for her to be right now. But that's the sort of bland, patronizing stuff teachers would say to you, so I didn't bother.

"You were pretty cool, by the way," I said instead, thinking a compliment was the best way to stop him thinking bleak thoughts. "I know I swam down to Rachel first, but *you* were the one who mostly carried her to the surface. You must take after your dad!"

TJ was silent for a second, but I think that's because he was well chuffed to be compared to his dad, who was a stuntman in Hollywood. TJ didn't see or hear from him very often, but you could tell he idolized him, the way he wouldn't let his mum take his father's framed photo off the wall.

"It was pretty easy lifting Rachel — she weighs about as much as a bag of crisps. She's so skinny, that's probably all she eats in a week!"

Good . . . he sounded a bit cheerier already, happily indulging in a healthy dose of black humour. I needed to keep this going somehow: and then an idea fluttered into my mind.

"Tomorrow . . . me and you, we should do something fun, something stupid, just have a laugh," I told him, realizing it was my turn to cheer *him* up, just as he'd tried to do for me earlier, when he'd spoiled my picture.

"Like what?"

"Like never mind. Like, just meet me tomorrow morning at ten, round at Sugar Bay, at Joseph's house. OK?"

"Er . . . OK," TJ mumbled warily.

Two seconds later, with a still-purring Peaches

in my arms, I headed off to play a game of Hunt
The Camera, wondering where exactly Mum
might have tidied it away, to keep it safe from
Dad's frantic DIYing and my little brothers'
tendency to pick up and throw anything that
wasn't nailed down. . .

CHAPTER 4

The Fake Fairy Photo Project

Ethereal: delicate, light as air, hazy.

Auntie V had used the word "ethereal" when she'd spoken about the faked fairy photos on the phone last night. The word had stuck in my mind, mainly 'cause I didn't know for sure what it *meant*.

Luckily, I came across the dictionary in the same drawer I found the camera (along with Mum's make-up bag, a set of sharp knives and a glass ornament that my Granny Stansfield had given us that looked *way* too breakable to put on show anywhere near itchy toddler fingers).

"How about . . . *here*!" said TJ.

With a cheeky grin, he plonked one of the paper fairies on a stick next to a sign the council had put up on the rusted railings, announcing the demolition of the old house later in the summer. A spray-painted tag (belonging to someone called "Oi!" by the looks of it) covered most of the council's waffle now. And in what little space there was left, another someone had felt-penned a swear word.

"Yeah, *right!*" I grinned back. "Somehow I *don't* think that'll give our photos the perfect atmosphere, d'you?"

I was tired but wired this morning. I'd stayed up late last night, painting convincingly delicate, light as air, hazy fairies. Course I had one already made – the "spoiled" painting rolled up and plonked in the bin looked perfect for mine and TJ's Fake Fairy Photo Project. With all the hard edges of my ninja fairy blurred and softened, it looked much more like a traditional airy-fairy fairy, if you see what I mean.

And so did the rest of the new paintings now, even though I hadn't managed to train Peaches to do his fancy trick again. Instead of him whooshing his hairy tail over my watery, watercolour efforts, I'd improvised and used one of my parents' house-painting brushes for that same smudgy, soft focus effect. Then, when they'd dried this morning, I'd carefully cut around each fairy, and taped them to thin, green garden stakes, so me and TJ could position them wherever we wanted.

And where we were positioning them now

was the garden of the dilapidated old mansion at Sugar Bay.

How come I'd thought about doing the photos here, instead of my own back garden? Well, *first* it was because this particular overgrown garden was overgrown with pretty, picturesque stuff like roses, ivy and foxgloves, unlike my garden at home, which was just a tangle of weeds, more weeds and mean plants with spikes.

The other reason was because my latest batch of fairies looked a lot like the one in the fragile framed picture on the wall of my den. *That* picture had been painted by Elize Grainger in the garden of our cottage. Miss Grainger had lived there as an old lady, but she'd grown up here at Joseph's house, which made it feel kind of spookily fitting to do our photos in the very garden that Elize would have played in zillions of years ago. (Well, OK, more like a century and a half ago, which is *practically* a zillion, give or take a year or two.)

"Where'd you get the sticks from?" asked TJ, as his sister Ellie happily danced around, waving one of my efforts like it was a wand.

"£1.99 from Woolies for a pack of ten. They're plant supports or something. Now try sticking that one next to those roses –"

"Oww!"

"– and watch out for the thorns!"

Rubbing his elbow, TJ went ahead and thrust the stick into the ground.

"Can you move a branch of that bush thing over, so you can't see the stick?" I asked, squinting into the viewfinder.

The image was pretty much perfect – apart from the collection of ugly-bug caravans sitting hunched up on the rock above the house and Sugar Bay.

Still, if I moved the camera a couple of centimetres over, then the horrible Seaview Holiday Homes should disappear nicely. . .

"Is that OK?" asked TJ, still fluffing up the bushy branch.

"Yep – that's great," I told him, watching his hand vanish from view, so that all that was left was a dainty fairy, dancing above the leaves.

I was just about to click the button when a large hairy head lunged into shot, sniffing at the camera.

"Bob! C'mere! Get out of the picture!" TJ ordered his bear of a dog. "Sorry, Stella!"

Actually, Bob wasn't the only animal interested in what we were doing. A seagull was sitting on the windowsill of what used to be a grand ballroom in Joseph's house, his beady yellow eyes watching our every move. No other seagull would be so brazen as to hang out so close (there were plenty of others whirling on salt-tinged slip-streams above our heads), and no other seagull looked so much like a cartoon brought to life (it was something about its crooked beak, slightly crossed eyes and clown-sized webbed feet). It *had* to be the psycho seagull – the one that Mrs S-T fed fairy cakes to, and the one that used to dive-bomb TJ – until TJ bribed him with more cake. Perhaps he was hoping we'd brought nibbles.

"Hey, that reminds me," I began, as TJ wrestled a reluctant Bob out of shot. "When we've done this, we should go inside the house and take a snap of the chandelier for posterity. Just in case Sam and his gang come back and wreck it for good."

A shiver wriggled down my spine. It had been horrible to hear those tinkles and crashes as the boys hurtled rocks at the beautiful crystal chandelier on Sunday.

"Don't think they'll be doing *that* in a hurry," said TJ, giving his pet a pat on the bum and sending him galumphing off to play with Ellie. "When I was walking Bob last night I bumped into this guy Jack I know from school. He said

Sam and that lot got a warning from the police: they do the *slightest* thing wrong from now on – even just *littering* or something – and the police are going to come down hard on them."

"Good," I said with a nod, taking a photo fast, before Bob bounded back for another sniff, or Ellie skipped into shot. "Right, how about doing one of a few of the fairies together?"

"Like a flock of fairies?" TJ suggested, his smile wide.

(The whole fairy thing might have been a bit girlie for him, but when I explained the Fake Fairy Photo Project to TJ when we met up this morning, he was *well* into the idea of the faking part. Which is typically boy-ish, when you think about it; boys are always into the slightly *twisted* side of things. It's like when you see a rabbit that's been squished by a car at the side of the road – it makes girls want to cry while boys just want to poke it with a stick.)

"Yeah – let's get a flock of fairies happening – maybe over by those lupins. . ."

As TJ gathered up the flock and headed over to the tall, wildly coloured flowers I'd pointed out, I decided to ask him something.

"TJ. . ."

"Uh-huh?"

"Yesterday, before what happened with Rachel happened, why were her and her friends acting so rude?"

I could practically hear Rachel's girlie voice grating in my head, and see her friend's sly grin as she bent down to quiz me.

"Because they think they're 'it'," he shrugged, planting the first of the fairies in place. "'Cause they swan about school thinking they're 'it'; they swan around town thinking they're 'it', and everyone tiptoes around them like they're something special."

"But that doesn't make sense!" I frowned. "Just because you're a bunch of girls who happen to be pretty and popular, what right does that give you to be rude and horrible?"

"*Duh!*" TJ laughed. "Because when you're pretty and popular like that lot, you don't *have* to be nice. You don't live in the real world. It just doesn't occur to you to *bother* with being nice, 'cause stuff just happens like magic for you anyway."

As he spoke, TJ rammed each fairy into position with so much force they started fluttering.

"What d'you mean, stuff just happens?" I asked TJ, hoping he wasn't spiking any innocent worms down there.

45

"What I mean is, if you're Rachel or Kayleigh or Brooke or Hazel, then people will *always* want you at their parties; guys will *always* want to go out with you; everyone will *always* want to be in your hip little gang. . . So girls like them don't waste time with dull things like thinking before they speak, the way the rest of us have to. They just go right ahead and say or do whatever pops into their empty little heads."

Wow. They'd *really* hurt TJ at one point or another (or *several* others); you could tell from the way he spat that little speech out.

"They've got a name for you, haven't they?" I guessed, hoping I wasn't hitting too raw a nerve.

"Yep – Beanie Boy."

Beanies . . . small and cute cuddly toys. So it wasn't the *harshest* name Rachel and co could have come up with, but if they said it to him with the same sarky-edged sniggers they'd used when it came to talking to *me*, then I could see why it would get your hackles up. (Whatever a hackle is . . . I've never been very sure.)

"Hey, that looks great, exactly how you've got them," I said suddenly, bypassing any comment on TJ's nickname now that I'd seen how cool (and convincing) the flock of fairies was looking.

"Yeah?" mumbled TJ proudly, backing away

from his handiwork as I came in close for a shot.

"Oh, yeah; I got it. But I'll take another couple of pictures 'cause it's absolutely per –"

I heard the flapping before I saw the psycho seagull try and perch himself on one of the fairies. Then it all unfolded through my viewfinder: the paper fairy crumpling beneath the weight of the seagull; the seagull tumbling in an ungainly pile of wings, scrawny legs, and squawking *straight* into the lupins and long grass; Bob thundering and barking up close, thinking the seagull wanted to play. (Fat chance – it probably wanted to poke Bob's eyes out, either through fear or shame at being caught looking so stupid.)

"BOB! *OFF!*" yelled TJ, holding his excitable dog by the collar long enough for the gull to flap away with only a few fluttering feathers left behind – oh, and *lots* of crushed fairies.

Well, the Fake Fairy Photo Project hadn't lasted too long. But it *had* been kind of fun, and it *had* cheered TJ up this morning, I guess.

"Don't worry, TJ, I've probably got enough photos as it is," I said quickly, spotting him staring open-mouthed at what were now just scraps of paper on sticks. I didn't want him coming over all guilty, just 'cause his dog and his stalker seagull had caused the destruction.

"Stella!" squeaked a small voice by my side.

"What's up, Ellie?"

TJ's kid sister – all blonde curls, big blinking eyes and slightly snotty nose – gazed up at me earnestly.

"The photos of the fake fairies . . . what are you going to do with them?"

"That," I replied, "is a very good question, Ellie."

Which I didn't have the answer to, 'cause I'd never thought any further than how cool it would be to copy what the original long-time-ago girls had done.

Good grief, a snotty-nosed, five-year-old had spotted a not-so-tiny flaw in my project.

That was *almost* as embarrassing as being a seagull who's rubbish at perching. . .

Chapter 5

Karaoke uh-oh. . .

"*One two . . . one two . . . ONE TWO . . . ONE TWO!!*"

"What *is* that?" I asked, staring round the crowded café in search of the boomy voice.

"Sounds like Phil – the guy who owns the place," said TJ. "Maybe he's installing a sound system so he can hassle his waitresses more easily. '*Amber! Can you wipe up that dollop of runny egg from table three, please!*' '*Muriel, can you take an order from that gang of thugs up at the back!*'"

What TJ was saying would have been funnier, if his former so-called mates – i.e. Sam and the rest of them – hadn't been sitting up at the back of the café. Luckily, they seemed to be happy to ignore us, and that was absolutely fine by me.

Bleep!

"Oh, a text," I mumbled, fumbling in my pocket for my mobile.

"Who's it from?"

"My friend Neisha from back home," I told TJ once I'd checked out the view panel.

How funny – I'd accidentally called London home, even though it technically wasn't any more.

In West End – just bot Usher's CD. We're all going 2 TopShop next. Wot u up 2? Luv Neish xx

OK, so my old friends back in London must be hanging out on Oxford Street, trailing around HMV with its giant video screens and pumping music, before going along to the huge, vast, *palace* of clothes that is the Oxford Circus branch of TopShop, where there'd be *more* giant video screens and pumping music. That sounded pretty good.

What *I* was doing was pretty good too, in its own way, but it was hardly like buying R'n'B CDs and casually mooching through mountains of the latest fashions. To be honest, I didn't know if my old friends would get it.

Taking it easy in sunshine, with my mate TJ, I texted Neisha back.

(Doing a Fake Fairy Photo Project with my mate TJ. And his kid sister's kicking about with us too, not to mention his dog. See? The truth just wouldn't come out right in a text. . .)

Sounds good! Is he cute, Lauren wants to know?

In a way, I texted straight back, feeling my cheeks go pink and hoping TJ was too busy spreading the photos out on the table to notice. I mean, I *was* telling the truth – TJ *was* cute in a way. In a small, cuddly, Beanie way, but I'd never be so rotten as to say that (or text that) in front of him.

Frankie says hi & she misses u. We all do!!!

Miss u all 2. Gotta go. . .

I signed off, knowing I'd better, before I got all misty-eyed for my old friends and old life and dripped all over the snaps I'd just spent my pocket money getting processed.

"I like *that* one," said Ellie, catching my attention as she squidged a dainty, sticky finger on to one of the fake fairy photos.

The Shingles café this afternoon was pretty busy, but me, TJ and Ellie had managed to snaffle the table by the window when a bunch of holidaymakers got up to leave. Maybe the reason they'd cleared off had a *tiny* bit to do with the fact that the three of us – plus Bob – had stood on the pavement outside, *right* in front of the plate-glass window, blocking their view of the sea and staring down at their empty plates.

OK, so we guilt-tripped them into leaving, I admit it. Whatever, while TJ ordered Bob to "SIT!" (and Bob looked offended), me and Ellie had nipped in and nabbed the table, just as Amber – the world's grumpiest teenage waitress – wiped it clean enough to put our newly printed photos down on.

"I quite like that one too, Ellie," I nodded. "The only thing is, it's got Bob's nose in it."

Right in it – there was just this fuzzy dark blob with two matching darker blobs sniffing at the camera lens.

"That's why I *like* it," said Ellie, with a definite nod and a slurp of her milkshake.

Me and TJ still hadn't figured out the answer to Ellie's question this morning, i.e. what exactly we were going to do with the pics we were gawping at. But at least we'd dropped them in at Snappy Snaps and had them printed up – that was a start.

"They look great!" said TJ enthusiastically, leaning over and studying the images of shimmery, not-quite-there fairies nestling among the ivy and the wild roses.

"Yeah, they do, don't th –"

Something had made TJ glance up sharply, and that something made me stop in mid-sentence. A chilly breeze had just blown in through the open café door in the shape of Rachel and her three buddies.

They stood there scanning the crowded room for non-existent spare tables, their eyes flickering over us without registering us at all. As far as three of the girls went, I couldn't care less if they looked our way or not. But as for *Rachel* acting like we were any old nobodies. . .

"'Hey, thanks a million, you guys!!'" muttered TJ under his breath, sarcasm dripping from his every word. "'For not letting me drown and everything yesterday!'"

"What *is* her problem?" I whispered, stunned at being blanked by a person whose life we'd saved and three witnesses to the fact we'd done it. It wasn't like I wanted a medal or anything; I just wouldn't have minded being treated like I *existed*.

"What's whose problem?" Ellie burst out loudly, stopping her slurping long enough to embarrass us. And pick her nose.

"Shhhh, Ellie!" TJ hushed his sister, before getting back to his dark mutterings with me. "I'm not going to let her get away with blanking us."

"Huh? Why? What are you going to do?" I asked worriedly. I might resent being treated like I was a lowly fleck of dust, but I didn't fancy getting into a fight over it. Plus there was only two (and a half) of us and four of them, and they all had lethal-looking false nails glued to their fingertips.

"Hey, Rach!" TJ called out.

Because of the hubbub of chat in the café, Rachel didn't seem to hear him. Or more likely, she was pretending she *couldn't* hear him.

"Does she like being called 'Rach'?" I mumbled, thinking it sounded very buddy-ish to shorten it like that, specially since TJ and Rachel weren't buddies.

"Nope. That's why I'm calling her that!" TJ grinned wickedly at me. "RACH! HEY, RACH!!"

"Hmm?" Rachel frowned his way, as if she couldn't quite figure out what her and TJ could possibly have to talk about.

"What happened yesterday?" said TJ, turning the volume on his voice down a little. "Are you all right?"

"Sure," she shrugged in response, then turned away, conversation concluded as far as she was concerned.

"I give up," TJ muttered darkly. "She might be as skinny as a cotton bud but she's still a total waste of space. . ."

Three thoughts whizzed round my brain at the same time:

1) I was relieved that TJ wasn't about to start a (very public) fight.

2) Rachel was *seriously* ungrateful.

3) I'd just heard that hint of a lisp again when she'd said "sure". . .

"Is she lisping?" I whispered, as I watched the four girls grab spare chairs and settle themselves down at a table where a girl was sitting on her own, reading.

"Yeah, but I think she does it on purpose, to try and sound cute or something," TJ snarled.

I didn't think so. As the not-so-proud owner of an occasional speech impediment of my very own, I knew nobody ever *wants* to stammer or lisp or struggle to pronouce their "r"s or whatever.

"Hey, don't go starting to feel *sorry* for her!" said TJ, raising his eyebrows at me and reading my mind. "Whether that lispy thing is real or not, she's just *mean* – like the rest of them. Look at what they're doing to Tilda!"

Tilda? OK – so she must be the book-girl at the table. I'd seen her round town before, looking like a cross between a goth and a ballerina (a gotherina?) in her black eyeliner, black T-shirt, and pink tutu. Right now she was getting the staring, silent treatment from the three girls who were Kayleigh, Brooke and Hazel. Meanwhile Rachel just sat back, twizzled a serviette between her fingers, and gazed around the room like a queen surveying her court.

Book-girl, or the gotherina, or Tilda or whatever she called herself, finally got the message: she was being moved on. Yeah, so we'd sort of done the same thing to the holidaymakers. But then they had obviously finished their food and were just taking up space, and in no *way* did we give them the dirty scowls Kayleigh, Brooke and Hazel were giving the weird goth/book/whatever girl.

Leaving behind her half-finished muffin, she snapped her book closed loudly and – with a screech of chair legs on lino – stomped out.

The second she'd gone, Rachel and co pulled their chairs in closer and carried on surveying the room like they owned it. *And* started picking at the left-behind muffin.

"Tell me again which one's which," I asked TJ. "And *don't* look at them while you tell me or they'll know we're talking about them and put a curse on us. . ."

"*Who'll* put a curse on us? Are there witches in here?!" Ellie piped up in a loud panic.

"Shhhhh!!" TJ urged his sis. "We're just joking around! Go and pat Bob through the glass or something!"

Doing as she was told, Ellie slipped off her seat and started doing pretend-stroking along Bob's furry back. Call it freaky, but Bob seemed to like it, leaning in closer to the window and drooling happily.

"OK. So let's start with Rachel, even though you already know her. Rachel Riley: pretty, long dark hair, stupid girlie voice, nearly drowned, totally ungrateful," TJ began breezily, now that Ellie was occupied. "Kayleigh Smith: prettyish, snub-nose, likes to think she's as gorgeous as Rachel but isn't."

Kayleigh had been the one who came out with the "tan" remark at the pool yesterday. I liked her the least of all four girls already, even ungrateful Rachel.

"Brooke Gilbert: blonde, always walks like she thinks she's on a catwalk, but she looks more like a kid that's filled its nappy. Hazel Crossland: light-brown hair, just sniggers along and agrees with whatever the others say 'cause she's got no personality of her own. That enough for you?"

"Yep," I nodded, getting a pretty good (i.e. pretty bad) idea of all four girls from TJ's short and sharply pointed descriptions.

"HEY, NICE PICTURES!!!"

Me, TJ, Ellie – and probably the whole of the café, including chefs out the back on their break – jumped out of our skin at that ear-splitting announcement.

"OOPS!" yelled Phil, the café owner, leaning over us with a microphone in his hand. "SORRY, IS THAT A BIT LOUD? I'LL JUST SWITCH IT OFF. Is that better?"

"Definitely!" said TJ, wincing at the squealing feedback whine the mike suddenly gave off.

"These photos – they're great! Fascinating! Did you two do them?"

Phil was as wide as two people, with a smile to match. His dark hair was receding on his head, but was growing up his chest and trying to escape over the top of the neck of his white T-shirt.

"Yep, I helped set it up – all those fake fairies I mean," TJ explained, doing my talking for me again, "but Stella came up with the idea, and took the pictures!"

"Wow . . . they look so real!" Phil muttered, picking one up and frowning his dark eyebrows at it. "Tell you what; you should send these anonymously to the local paper, see if they print 'em and do a story about 'em!"

My heart skipped a beat or twelve. *That's* what we could do – we could copy the original 1900s girls, not just by imitating their fairy snaps, but by getting them published as the real thing!

"They don't look that real to *me*," said a snippy voice all of a sudden.

"Me neither!"

The first voice belonged to Kayleigh, who was peeking over Phil's shoulder with a sour-puss look on her face. The second voice belonged to Hazel, who was automatically agreeing with Kayleigh, just like TJ had said she would. All four girls seemed to have left the table they'd bullied the goth girl away from and had been making their way to the newly vacated one next to ours, nearer the window.

"Anyway, what's the point of sending them to the local paper and hoping they think they're real?" Brooke chipped in, curiosity getting the better of her.

"For fun?" TJ suggested, staring daggers at her.

"But if the papers printed a story saying they thought these were real," said Kayleigh, scrunching up her mean little snub-nose, "we'd just phone them up and tell them we heard you saying they were faked!"

Phil looked at Kayleigh like she'd just popped all the balloons at a kids' party out of spite, and in a way, that's exactly what she'd done.

"OK, OK, GUYS," he burst out, flicking the switch on his mike to "on" and deliberately yelling a little louder as he passed close to Kayleigh's ear. "HOW ABOUT SOMEONE DOES ME A

59

FAVOUR? NEXT WEEK IS THE PORTBAY GALA, AND WE'RE GOING TO BE HAVING KARAOKE COMPETITIONS HERE AT THE SHINGLE CAFÉ EVERY NIGHT TO CELEBRATE. SO HAVE I GOT A VOLUNTEER TO GIVE ME A SONG TO TEST THE GEAR OUT?"

"Ahh!" gasped a little voice, as Ellie stopped doing her dog-patting mime and scrambled to her feet.

"Oh no. . ." mumbled TJ, dropping his head in his hands.

"But I could sing 'Over the Rainbow'!" Ellie whispered excitedly to her brother. "Or that song off the yoghurt ad that I like!"

But someone had beaten Ellie to it. While she was still whispering possibilities in her embarrassed brother's ear, Rachel had said something to Phil, and was now heading towards a corner of the café where two big speakers and a TV screen were stacked.

"TJ – check it out!" I murmured.

Lifting his head from his hands, TJ was just in time to see Rachel smile smugly, flick her long dark hair and bat her almond eyes in the direction of Sam and his gang (yuck).

"Aw! Not fair!" whined Ellie, spotting that her

moment was gone and slumping back down in her chair.

"Never mind, Ellie – bet she's not as good as you!" I whispered, thinking of Rachel's girlie squeak.

Er. . .

It only took about ten seconds of Kylie's "Can't Get You Out of my Head" to realize that if Rachel swapped her designer tracksuit bottoms for hotpants and dyed her dark hair blonde, she could make a fortune as Kylie's double. Her high-pitched speaking voice might get on your nerves, but her singing voice was sweet and breathy, the slight hint of a lisp the only thing that stopped it from being pretty much perfect.

And it wasn't just all of us in the café who were gobsmacked; people were stopping outside on the pavement, peering in, probably convinced that a small Australian celebrity must have taken time out of her busy schedule to jet to Portbay for her holidays.

But even when they realized it wasn't the real Kylie, they still stood there gawping, watching this pretty girl with the amazing voice, and nearly treading on Bob, who had to keep shuffling his hairy self about to make way for them all.

In fact, between the café customers, the staff

and the holidaymakers on the pavement, Rachel must have had an audience of about forty or so people (and a dog).

Which meant an awful lot of people saw her suddenly start trembling.

And then rolling her eyes.

And then fainting with a clatter on to the café floor, where she shook and shuddered like she'd been hit by lightning.

Like yesterday at the pool, it had all happened in a nano-second. And in the following nano-seconds, I suddenly became aware of everyone's reactions. Yesterday, all I'd seen was Rachel's friends' horrified faces, before I dived underwater. This time I heard all the shouts, shock and murmurings – from inside and outside the café – even if it was a muddle of voices all overlapping each other.

"Oh, no!!" [an old lady at a table of old ladies]

"Has she fainted?" [a holidaymaker in the open doorway]

"Rachel – are you OK?" [Phil the café owner]

"What's going on? What's happened to that girl?" [someone outside]

"Woof!" [Bob]

"Is she going to be all right?" [Muriel, the older waitress]

"AMBER – CALL AN AMBULANCE!" [Phil, using the mike]

"Oh my God, has she been electrocuted?" [the mum of a family sitting close to us]

"RACHEL! CAN YOU HEAR ME?" [Phil, forgetting he still had the mike in his hands]

"Shouldn't someone put her in the recovery position?" [another holidaymaker hovering uselessly in the doorway]

"Excuse me, I'm a nurse!" [someone from the pavement squeezing through]

"Is she dead?" [Ellie]

"Ha ha ha ha ha ha!" [Sam's gang]

I felt numb with shock. Not just 'cause of seeing Rachel fainting or collapsing again or whatever, and not just 'cause of Sam's gang *laughing* (the morons), but 'cause once again, Rachel's friends were sitting frozen, silent and horrified.

"No, she's not *dead*, Ellie," I heard TJ reassure his sister.

"Is she *pretending* to be dead, then?"

"No, it's not that. . ."

I tuned out of TJ's explanations and stared stupefied at Kayleigh, Hazel and Brooke. Why weren't they running over to check on their best mate? Why did they look kind of repulsed, like they were watching something gross like a bowel transplant or slug-eating competition?

"Can I go and look at her, and *check* she's not dead?"

"*No*, Ellie, and she's *not* dead," said TJ, hurriedly throwing down enough coins to cover our drinks and scooping up the photos. "Let's go, Stella – Ellie's a bit freaked, and there're other people around to save Rachel today."

Yeah, plenty of people; *not* including her mates. And with mates as useless as shoes made of custard, I suddenly felt kind of sorry for Rachel.

(And yeah, I *know* I'm a mug. . .)

CHaPTeR 6

How to get your head bitten off in one easy lesson

". . .and then – OW! Jamie, *careful!*"

"What's he doing?" asked Frankie, sounding like she was sitting right beside me on the beach instead of in her living room in North London.

"Whacking me on the shin with his spade," I mumbled, as Jamie bent over to kiss my leg better – then spluttered as he got a mouthful of sand.

"You should wear padding around your brothers!" giggled Frankie. "Anyway, get on with what you were telling me."

"Oh, yeah. Anyway, she just went *splat.*"

"*Again?!* What did you do?"

"Well, nothing, 'cause this time the café owner—"

"Hold on. Mum's trying to butt in."

In the background I heard faint mumblings – Frankie must have put her hand over the phone.

"Mum's asking if Rachel's all right now."

Frankie sighed when she spoke, but she should've been used to her nice mum chipping in all the time. Aunt Esme always acted like any conversation was up for grabs, joining in with people at bus stops when she got half a chance.

"I don't know, 'cause—"

"Hold on, Stell. What're you saying, Mum?"

Frankie didn't put her hand over the receiver this time, and although I couldn't make out the exact words Aunt Esme was saying, her familiar, warm, booming voice zapped me from being a thirteen-year-old girl sitting on a beach many motorways away from Kentish Town, to a little kid in Frankie's flat being hugged to death by my lovely childminder (i.e. Aunt Esme).

"Stell, Mum's asking what happened both times – before Rachel collapsed."

"Well. . ." I began, feeling myself shiver at the uncomfortable memories. "She sort of went very still, and then just started trembling – even her eyelids – and then she fainted and started twitching really badly when she was unconscious."

"Stell says the girl went all trembly and stuff."

Aunt Esme (who wasn't a real aunt, but loved me like she was) obviously got enough, from Frankie's weary shortened version to make some kind of sense of it, 'cause I could hear her chattering again.

"Stell, Mum says she thinks it sounds like . . . what d'you call it again, Mum? Oh, right – epil . . . something."

"*Epilepsy!*" I heard Aunt Esme roar goodnaturedly.

"Yeah . . . that," Frankie mumbled.

To be honest, I wasn't really sure what epilepsy *was* exactly, but if Aunt Esme was convinced about it, then *I* was convinced. After all, she was the one who took splinters out of my knee when I was three, while Mum and Dad worked full-time at their fancy magazine company. And that practically made her a *doctor*, as far as I was concerned.

"Stella – can I call you back later, when Mum isn't trying to earwig all the time?"

"Oi, Miss Cheeky Monkey – I *heard* that!" Aunt Esme called out somewhere in the background.

"Sure," I smiled, missing the loud, easy banter that went on non-stop round at Frankie's place.

And then my faraway friend was gone, and I was left mulling over the whole epil-whatsit stuff.

Well, I mulled for a whole second at least, till I noticed a seagull circling in low, flapping circles along the beach. And right below it was TJ (short

67

and ambling), Bob (huge and panting) and Ellie (small and skipping).

"YAYYYY!" yelled Jake and Jamie, throwing their spades down on my legs as they both made a shrieking beeline for Ellie and Bob.

At the noise my brothers made, the swirling seagull turned sharply and flapped off to the safety of a lamppost on the prom. Bob looked like he wished he could do the same, now that Jake had his furry head in a stranglehold cuddle and Jamie was trying to climb on his back like he was a Shetland pony.

"Let me guess . . . Frankie?" said TJ, nodding at the phone I still had tucked between my chin and my shoulder as he lifted a wriggling Jamie off Bob's hairy back.

TJ was getting used to the regular texts and calls that pinged back and forth between me and Frankie in particular, plus Neisha, Parminder, Lauren and Eleni.

"Yep. Her mum said something interesting. . ."

"Hey, look – it's Rachel," TJ interrupted me. "Not looking too happy, is she?"

I spun my head around to see what TJ could, and there was Rachel, storming out of her mum's gift shop on the prom and running across the road.

"What's she trying to do – get herself killed?" said TJ, frowning at the sound of cruising cars parping their horns at her. "Whatever it looked like yesterday, she can't have been *that* ill – she seems pretty OK now!"

I put my hand over my eyes, shielding the sun for a proper look at Rachel. She didn't look pretty OK to me; she looked pale and tired and angry. The way she'd flopped down on to the stairs to the beach just now and started agitatedly hammering numbers into her mobile, you could tell she wasn't exactly having an excellent day.

"Frankie's mum says she thinks Rachel's got epilepsy."

"Yeah? I s'pose it *could* be that," TJ nodded thoughtfully. "What is it again?"

"Don't know exactly – I'll have to look it up on the internet later," I mumbled, watching Rachel intently as she pressed her mobile to her ear, biting the side of her mouth hard. After listening to something or someone for a few seconds, Rachel angrily thumped her index finger on what had to be the end-call button, and dropped her head on to her knees.

"I'm going to go and see if she's all right," I said, trying to stand up, but forgetting I had a mound of sand on each leg and falling back down again.

"Speak to her?" laughed TJ. "What's the point? She'll just knock you back, like she did yesterday, remember?"

"Yeah, but I've still got to *try*," I told him, feeling nervous about approaching Rachel, but more worried I'd feel like a heartless git if I didn't. "Can you look after the boys for a minute?"

I vaguely heard TJ say yes, but I wasn't really listening, if you see what I mean. I was too busy psyching myself up as I padded across the shifting hot sands towards Rachel, in case she felt like telling me where to go.

So *why* did I feel drawn to try and help a girl like her? Well, apart from knowing she was ill, I knew deep inside it was because we had something in common. It might only be a hated speech impediment, but it was something. Something I could relate to more than anyone else she knew, I bet. . .

"Um, hi!" I began, looking down on her hunched shoulders.

Rachel raised her head. She still looked pretty, but in the way frail heroines look in novels like *Oliver Twist*, when they're dying of TB or consumption or potato famine or whatever. And then there was the bruise on her cheekbone, that matched the bluey-purply bruises on her right

70

arm and on her knee as well. For half-a-second I panicked that Rachel might really be dying too, then I remembered that she'd been taken to hospital twice, and they'd hardly keep sending her home if she was on her last legs.

"Um . . . just w-w-wondered if you were OK," I asked, my old nervy stammer creeping in.

Suddenly the tired sadness left Rachel's pale (and bruised) face and was replaced by – oo-er – fury. (Was it too late to turn and run?)

"OK? *How* can I be OK?" she said shrilly, her girlie voice taking on a whole new tone.

"I-I-I don't kn—"

"Would *you* be OK if you were told you might have epilepsy?"

There was the slight lisp again, but it was hardly the time to point out our common problem, when Rachel seemed kind of overwhelmed by problems just now.

"Well, no I wou—"

"Would *you* be OK if you were told that the hospital wants to do lots of scary tests on you?"

"I-I-I guess no—"

"Would *you* be OK if your best mates had gone weird on you, and wouldn't talk to you, like you had *leprosy* or something?"

I was about to try and stammer off another

no, but Rachel obviously didn't want to hear it. Picking herself up off the step she turned and ran off, dodging her way between the traffic on the prom again.

Now that I'd had my head bitten off, TJ would be dying to say "told you so".

Or maybe not.

When I hurried back over to him, his first words were, "Help! Please!" Which wasn't a great surprise considering Jake, Jamie, Ellie and Bob had managed to bury everything except his head and the toe of one Converse trainer in the sand in the few minutes I'd been gone. . .

Welcome to Gloomsville

Outside in the blazing sunshine, tourists were happily licking Soleros as they strolled around, gawping at shells with "Hurry back to Portbay!" painted on them and getting sunstroke.

Inside The Vault, no one could *ever* get sunstroke, since it was painted entirely in black and rock posters were plastered over the window. And no tourists *ever* dared to venture in here – it was a local (records and vintage comics) shop for local people, hidden down a side street.

After Mum came and met us down at the beach and took the twins home for their nap, me, TJ, Ellie and Bob had wandered up here. Not that TJ had let Ellie and Bob inside – that would be *way* too uncool. At the moment, they were sitting happily on the pavement outside, with their bribes of *Mad About Animals* magazine and a bag of chocolate buttons (they were sharing both, last time I peeked out and checked on them).

"But don't you feel just a *teeny* bit sorry for Rachel?" I said to TJ, as he flicked through the CD racks, like he'd been doing for the last ten minutes, without finding anything he liked.

I wished he'd hurry up. The one good thing about The Vault was the very cute guy (called Si) behind the sales desk, but there were several *bad* things about the shop. For a start, it was so gloomily dark in there that I kept thinking I'd gone blind, PLUS it was as hot as the inside of a toaster, AND the music was so loud that TJ could only hear me when I stood about five centimetres away from his ear.

"Nope," said TJ, with a firm shake of his head. "Rachel's an idiot. I know she's not well, but that doesn't mean she's not an idiot. Sorry."

I knew what TJ meant, but I kept hearing a tiny voice in my head say "poor Rachel!" every time I thought about her running off from me earlier. It wasn't so much that I felt sorry for her having epilepsy, it was more to do with her friends going frosty on her. And the lisp thing.

"But there's her lisp and everything!"

"Her lisp never stopped her being bitchy or gossipy about anyone *else*'s problems, so I don't see why that should make me feel sorry for her now!"

Fair enough. I didn't get referred to as "Beanie Boy" by Rachel and her former friends, I s'pose. I'd have to try to appeal to his sensitive side in a *different* way.

"But TJ, her mates have turned on her. *You* know how horrible it is to feel like an outsider, and so did I, when I first moved here!"

TJ stopped flipping and stared at me disbelievingly, like I was a very little kid who'd said something very, very dumb.

"Stella, the reason I feel like an outsider in this town is because of people like Rachel Riley and her gang taking the mickey out of me! And her and that lot didn't make *you* feel too welcome either, remember!"

"I guess so. . ." I shrugged, hating being told off (even if TJ was right) and spinning away from him.

I was thinking about waiting for him outside, and maybe scrounging a chocolate button if there were any left, when I noticed something.

Si – the cute assistant guy – was handing a used-looking tissue to someone who was either a) cowering behind the counter, or b) very small indeed.

Easing my way along the over-stuffed racks of CDs, I came to a casual stop at the vintage comics, and began to pretend to glance through one.

And then I saw her – Rachel – her tiny bum in her hipster tracky bottoms perched on a gift box of *Buffy the Vampire Slayer* videos. And she was crying.

Without wanting anyone to spot me, I ducked down, and hurried back, all doubled up, to TJ.

"Hey! Rachel's behind the counter! Crying! Why d'you think she's crying? And why do you think she's talking to that guy Si? Are they going out or something?"

I couldn't see it – Rachel wasn't the sort of girl who'd go out with a grungy, gothy rocker like this boy, no matter *how* cute his face was (apart from the pierced lip – *yeeeew*).

"Si is Rachel's brother," said TJ, staring down at me. "Hey, are you standing in a hole or something?"

I straightened up, just in time to see Rachel running out of the door, with a tissue clamped to her nose and her brother yelling, "Look, Rach – I'm sorry! I *was* listening! I just thought you blubbing like that would put off customers!"

For the second time today, I felt drawn to follow Rachel. And for the second time today, I knew that TJ would think I was wasting my time. . .

"Hi, Stella! Look at this poster of bunnies! They're really cute, aren't they?"

"I'll look at it in a second, Ellie," I called over my shoulder as I hurried along the narrow side street.

Rachel must be a fast runner – she'd disappeared around the corner and into the High Street, where I found myself now, halted and panting. I flicked my head one way – no sign. I flicked my head the other way, towards the sea, and saw her hurrying forward, waving.

"Kayleigh!" I heard her call out.

Yuck. Sure enough, coming towards her on the same side of the road were Kayleigh and her cronies. Rachel wouldn't be interested in little old me trying to comfort her now that *that* lot were in view.

Except . . . except they were blanking her. I saw Kayleigh mouth "C'mon – let's go!" before she led an unsmiling Brooke and Hazel across the road.

Meanwhile, Rachel seemed to be slowing her walk to a standstill, her head turned in disbelief as her ex-friends crossed the road in front of her as fast as their expensive trainers would take them.

My blood boiled – how could they treat her like that, leaving her confused and stumbling along the street? They could do it because they were shallow, heartless and ignorant. TJ had done the same to me not so long ago, when he was reluctantly hanging out with Sam's mean gang, and the thought of it still left a sour taste in my mouth, even though TJ had more than made it up to me since.

But with that recent memory pinging around my head, I knew that though Rachel was no friend of mine, I could no more leave her standing there like a dork than I could leave a tiny kitten stranded in the middle of a motorway.

A few short, fast strides took me right alongside Rachel.

"Keep walking," I told her, as I linked my arm in hers and propelled her along. "Don't look over at them and try not to look upset. Don't let them know they've hurt you."

From the corner of my eye I could see that Kayleigh, Brooke and Hazel's heads were all turned our way, wondering what on earth was going on.

"What are you doing?" Rachel frowned at me, obviously wondering what on earth was going on too. But still, she sped up her walking all the same.

"Saving your pride," I told her, plastering a big, fake smile on my face. "Now stop frowning and pretend to smile too!"

Seeing my point, Rachel forced something like a smile on her face.

But looking at her eyes, I didn't know whether she wanted to thank me or *kill* me. . .

Ready or not, here I come. . .

Luckily, Rachel didn't kill me. She didn't exactly thank me, either. In fact, she didn't say much of *anything* in those first few minutes, except, "I've got to get away!"

So I thought it was my duty to get her away – to here. To Sugar Bay. . .

"I can't climb up there! I'll get all dirty!"

"But you've come all this way – you've *got* to see it!"

I gazed down into the tangled garden, and saw Rachel frowning up at me. TJ was frowning too – at Rachel. Over on the right, Ellie and Bob were racing each other down to the sea, both of them wearing daisy chains around their necks.

"I can't do it!" said Rachel in a babyish voice, with a shake of her head. "I'd scuff my trainers – and I only just got them!"

TJ rolled his eyes.

"Look, just get on my back, OK?" he sighed,

80

bending over so Rachel could use him as a human stepladder.

She looked like she was trying to think of something else to protest about, and then gave up. With a sudden thump and an "oooof!" (from TJ), Rachel was up, levering herself through the huge empty window. Half a second later, TJ had joined us both.

"So this is it – Joseph's house!" I said almost proudly, if it was possible to be proud of an old, semi-derelict house that doesn't belong to you.

Rachel said nothing (she'd been doing a lot of that on the way over here), and instead scanned the room.

The breeze was perfectly timed; it made the grand(ish) chandelier tinkle softly. And as the cut-crystal swayed and danced in the soft afternoon shafts of sunlight, tiny rainbow twinkles flashed around the faded ballroom. It reminded me of the first time I ever came in here, and thought the twinkles were . . . well, something else, something much more magical and mysterious. A bit like deep down in the pool the other day, I guess.

I was pleased Rachel was seeing the old house like this. From the second I'd come across it, I'd loved it (even though it had spooked me out a bit), and I'd really wanted to show the place off.

On the way over here, Rachel had told us (practically the *only* thing she'd told us) that she'd never been inside Joseph's house, and hadn't visited Sugar Bay since she was a little kid, even though it was only fifteen minutes over the headland – past the caravans of the Seaview Holiday Homes – from town.

Now I could see her gazing around, her tears long dried, and I couldn't *wait* to hear what she had to say about it.

"Smells like something *died* in here."

As she wrinkled up her delicate nose, I didn't dare look TJ's way. Out of the corner of my eye I could see he'd stopped scuffing dustballs along with the toe of his trainer – he must've been *aching* to mouth "Told you so!" at me again. In fact, I could practically sense him zapping me that message via ESP.

"It's just kind of musty," I tried to suggest.

"Just kind of pongy, you mean!"

This wasn't going quite the way I'd hoped.

Earlier, after I'd rescued Rachel (from shame instead of drowning this time), she'd more-or-less silently let me lead her here, her hands stuffed in her pockets and her eyes facing down, watchful of her every step, in her expensive new trainers. TJ had said nothing much either. After catching us up on the street, him, Ellie and Bob followed me and Rachel, keeping a couple of wary metres in our wake.

I'd thought everything would change when we got inside Joseph's house; I'd thought Rachel might get excited, just like I had when I first discovered the place. For me, it had been as brilliant as finding a secret world behind a cupboard door. For Rachel, the place was as enchanting as a wheelie bin at the back of a supermarket.

"So who used to live here?"

"Well, this was the Graingers' house, of course. It's only called Joseph's house after their servant, isn't it?"

Rachel shrugged, like it was the first she'd heard of anything like that, even though the town's museum was full of the whole story, AND a replica of this exact same ballroom, in all its glory (just minus the chandelier).

"Guess it wasn't such a dump back in the old days. . ." she commented.

OK, now I was starting to think this had been a very *bad* idea.

I *had* been going to tell her about Elize Grainger, and the young servant boy from Barbados who'd been her playmate, and about the names I'd found scratched in the windowsill upstairs (*Elize & Joseph – friends for eternity*), but now I didn't think I'd bother.

"Maybe we should just go," I muttered glumly, heading for the window ledge.

"Stella!" TJ shouted out.

I turned in time to see Rachel swaying, her eyes wide and bright as car headlights. Around her upper body was a halo of those rainbow twinkles. It was as if the frantic flurrying of concerned fairies was the only thing holding her upright. . .

Uh-oh – Rachel was about to have one of her fits again and I was going *mad*.

"It's all right! I'm all right!" Rachel insisted, as me and TJ made a grab for her. "I'm not going to faint!"

The light outside had suddenly changed, I noticed – maybe a cloud had crept across the sun, and the rainbow twinkles had darted off to quiet, hidden corners of the house.

"Well . . . what's wrong with you, then?" TJ asked bluntly.

Rachel looked mortified, squirming on the spot.

"I can't tell you," she mumbled. "You'd think I was an idiot."

TJ thinks that already, I said to myself, in the privacy of my own head.

"But *something* made you go funny just now, Rachel."

At my words, Rachel began to bite the side of her mouth again, just like she had when I saw her on the beach this morning.

"If I tell you, you mustn't laugh."

I glanced at TJ, TJ glanced at me. Neither of us could think of anything to say but "OK".

"The last couple of days since I had my first fainting thing," Rachel began, watching us warily for stray giggles, "I've felt like I can *sense* things."

"Like what?" I asked, my heart racing, wondering if she was going to mention the twinkling; the twinkling that I had to keep convincing myself was just a bunch of tricks of the light.

"Like stupid stuff," Rachel answered me. "What song's going to come on the radio next. . . What dumb thing my lame-brain brother's going to say. . . What the 'doof-doof-doof' cliffhanger ending's going to be on *EastEnders*. . ."

TJ's shoulders started heaving, as he struggled to keep his giggles at bay.

"See? I *told* you it was stupid!" Rachel burst out angrily. "Mum didn't believe me when I told her

85

this morning, and neither did Kayleigh the other day!"

"So what did you sense just now?" I asked Rachel, wishing TJ was close enough for me to give him a subtle kick in the shins.

"You don't want to know. . . He's just going to laugh at me some more."

"Ignore him, Rachel! And *I* do want to know – please tell me!"

So many strange and spooky things had happened to me since I'd moved to Portbay (including one strange and spooky cat who'd moved in with me), that I was happy to hear that they happened to other people too.

Rachel seemed pretty dubious. But I guess if she'd fallen out with her friends and family, that meant she didn't have anyone much else apart from me (and TJ) to talk to right now.

"I felt like someone was playing hide 'n' seek in here. A girl in this big, puffy long dress was behind a big red curtain over there, giggling –"

Rachel pointed to a long, bare window. I knew that in the replica ballroom in the museum, there was a long red velvet curtain hanging at those same windows.

"– and a boy's voice was laughing and shouting, 'Ready or not, here I come!'"

A shiver rippled up my spine and back down again for luck. Had Rachel just "sensed" Elize and Joseph, the house's playmates from so long ago?

I didn't know. What I *did* know was that TJ wasn't giggling any more. . .

Chapter 9

Alien invasions and finger-crossings

"Lift!" grumbled Amber, the grumbliest, most miserable waitress in the history of cafés.

It was still Wednesday. It had felt like a really *loooonnngggg* day; seeing Rachel down on the beach, spotting her crying in The Vault, hearing her spook the living daylights out of us round at Sugar Bay. After that, Rachel had headed home, but me and TJ felt like we needed to soothe our frazzled brains with a long, cool drink.

"*Now*, please!" Amber grumbled some more, as our weary brains failed to respond quickly enough to her barked orders.

We did as we were told, lifting our elbows and glasses of iced Coke off the table while Amber flung a gingham paper tablecloth down.

"They always put tablecloths on at this time of day," TJ explained, as Amber hurried away without a thank you. "They think it makes the place look posh, for the evening crowd."

I quickly checked my watch; it was quarter to five – still a little while before my parents expected me home for tea.

"Y'know, this is a bit like what-do-you-call-it; that *déjà* thingy," TJ suddenly murmured, glancing around the caff. "That thing where you feel something's happened before?"

"Déjà vu," I told him, remembering asking my mum what that meant once. "Hey, you're not going all spooky on me too, are you?"

"No!" grinned TJ. "But it's funny we're sitting at the same table as we were yesterday, when Rachel was singing and everything."

He was right. Loads of things were identical. We might have had the "posh" tablecloth on and the café customers might be a bit thin on the ground till they started drifting in for burgers and stuff later, but plenty was the same. Yep, we were sitting in the window seat again. And there was Bob, steaming up the window with his doggy breath, waiting impatiently for us to hurry up. Over in the corner were the speakers and TV screen for the karaoke, where Ellie was now happily tap-dancing to some tune in her head (probably the song to the yoghurt ad she liked). Even Kayleigh and co were here, only they were sitting up at the back, thankfully well away from us. Though they were doing *plenty* of staring our way. . .

"So . . . do you think her epilepsy has made Rachel *psychic* or something?" I asked TJ, wondering if I sounded faintly mad saying that (I'd *have* to look up epilepsy on the computer when I got home).

"Maybe . . . but I had another idea!" said TJ, his eyes wide and earnest. "How about, she's tuning into alien frequencies! Maybe they've made her a receptor or something!"

"And maybe you read too many *Spider-man* comics," I said, raising one disbelieving eyebrow at him.

"No – honest! We've got cable TV at home and I've seen the most amazing documentaries about people being beamed into spacecraft, and they can't remember anything about it, they just know they've got some telepathic connection with aliens! Honest!"

Good grief, TJ was *such* a typical boy. Every single one of them (including my dad) *loved* that sci-fi stuff.

"TJ, if Rachel got sucked up inside an alien spaceship then I'm an *ostrich*."

Before me and TJ got to waffle more about alien spaceships, ostriches or even alien ostriches, we heard a familiar (loud) voice.

"HELLO, EVERYONE. HAVING A GOOD TIME?" Phil boomed into his mike with a big grin.

He was standing behind the counter with the mike in one hand and a burger flipper in the other. It was pretty obvious that the mike was like a new toy to him. Specially the way the waitresses rolled their eyes when he talked through it. He'd probably been fooling about with it all day and driving everyone mad.

"WELL? COME ON PEOPLE! I SAID, ARE YOU HAVING A GOOD TIME!!!"

Some holidaymakers at the table next to us called out "yes!" (except for the oldest of their two teenage daughters, who looked bored and mortified), backed up by Ellie's squealed "YESSSSS!!"

Just as well that lot replied, since the rest of the café's customers didn't bother – i.e. me and TJ, and Kayleigh and her crew.

"GLAD TO HEAR IT," beamed Phil. "SO, GIRLS – HOW'S YOUR FRIEND RACHEL DOING?"

That (loud) comment of Phil's was directed at Kayleigh, Brooke and Hazel of course. The family of holidaymakers turned and looked at the three of them too – I was pretty sure they'd been in here on Monday, when Rachel's seizure got the better of her singing (maybe they were staying up at the lovely Seaview Holiday Homes. . .).

And so how did Kayleigh, Brooke and Hazel answer Phil's question? By aiming blank looks and matching shrugs his way.

"GREAT. THANKS FOR THAT HEART-WARMING RESPONSE, GIRLS. I'M SURE RACHEL WOULD BE OVERWHELMED BY YOUR CONCERN."

"He's pretty funny, that guy!" I said, nodding at Phil, who was masking his sarcasm behind a cheeky grin and a casual flip of a burger.

"Well, they're so thick-skinned AND thick, they probably don't even *get* that Phil's having a go at them," TJ laughed dryly, with a quick nod in Kayleigh and co's direction.

"And they're not just thick-skinned and thick – they're horrible too," I muttered. "I mean, how can they go weird on their friend when she's ill, and then go completely cold on her when she's trying to tell them how nuts she's feeling?"

"I know. She doesn't deserve that."

"Omigod, TJ – you actually feel sorry for Rachel!" I laughed, catching him out.

"No, I don't."

"Yes, you do – admit it. Even if you just admit

to being a tiny, minuscule, hardly visible bit sorry for her!"

"OK, maybe," he admitted grudgingly. "Maybe I *do* feel a tiny, minuscule, hardly visible bit sorry for her. But just a tiny, minuscule, hardly visible bit!"

"I knew it! I *knew* you were a softie inside, like me!"

"Hmm," shrugged TJ. "But I'm probably going to regret saying I feel sorry for her."

"Don't be so gloomy," I joked him along. "Why would *that* happen?"

Underneath the table I kept my fingers crossed very, very tight. . .

ChAPTeR 10

Ho-hummmm. . .

Flicking through a few internet sites, I found myself listening to humming in stereo.

The first kind of hum was mechanical (coming from the computer hard drive) and the second was purr-able (coming from Peaches). He'd hopped up on the table and nicely hidden the mess of paper spread out all over it with his fluffy ginger fatness.

Tea hadn't been quite ready when I got in, so I'd come through to pootle around on the internet and see what I could find out about epilepsy. And maybe I was picking it up wrong, but the two main things I'd found out were. . .

1) epilepsy works like this: everybody has electrical charges in their brain, but with epilepsy, once in a while you get a sudden big *surge* of electricity, which is like a fuse blowing in a lamp or something.

2) the proper name for fits is seizures. People

often don't get any warning that they're about to
have a seizure – the first thing they know about it
is when they wake up on the ground. They can
have a splitting headache and feel really tired
afterwards. The seizures themselves can't really
hurt you too badly, it's more that you can hurt
yourself when you fall down.

Ping!

Aha! An e-mail from Frankie – nice timing.

Hi Stella!
What're you up to? I was hanging out with
Seb all afternoon, which was great, except
that Eleni gave me a really hard time about
it 'cause we were all meant to be getting the
bus to Brent Cross Shopping Centre, and I
totally forgot – urgh. I tried saying sorry but
Eleni was in one of those huffy moods of
hers where she's not up for listening.

I'd forgotten that Eleni could be like that. But
I guess me and my old mates all had our annoying niggles. Like Frankie could be too cocky
and flip about stuff, and Lauren could be
irritatingly dippy and vague. Then there was
Parminder's annoying habit of always outdoing
you ("You've got headache? Well, when I had that

terrible migraine. . ."), and Neisha could drive you crazy with that sniff, sniff, sniffing thing she does when she has a runny nose (can't the girl use a tissue?).

And then of course I knew I used to drive *them* mad by wimping out of stuff all the time, and being too shy to stand up for myself. If they could all see me now! (OK, so Frankie already had, when she was here visiting, and OK, so I'm not exactly fearless like Catwoman or something.)

I guess 'cause I managed to like all my friends even *with* their faults, same as they liked me with mine, I felt more inclined to give Rachel a chance. Specially since her own, supposed friends hadn't given her much of a chance. . .

Oops got to go – Mum's shouting that tea's ready. (Macaroni cheese with extra cheese – mmmm!)
Miss you ☹, but M8s 4eva ☺!
Frankie

I pressed an icon on the toolbar, and was just about to e-mail Frankie a reply, telling her about hanging out with Rachel today, when my own mum shouted that tea was ready.

"I'll save you something!" I promised Peaches,

giving his head a quick scratch. Not that Peaches looked in imminent need of more munchies – his fat, round belly was full of Felix, I reckoned.

"Er, nice tablecloth," I said, bounding from the computer to the kitchen in a few strides across bare floorboards. "Why've we gone posh though?"

With the glossy, floral cloth spread over our big pine table, it was like we were trying to outdo the Shingles cafe with their gingham paper efforts.

"Well, we haven't exactly gone *posh*," Mum grinned, taking a seat beside a steaming plate of lasagne. "It's more of a quick fix. I just got fed up with clearing cement and sawdust off the table every time we wanted to eat, so I thought it would be quicker just covering it up!"

"Your mum's a genius!" Dad laughed, dolloping spoonfuls of beans on to Jake and Jamie's plates, alongside their fishfingers.

Actually, Dad's hair and clothes were covered in so much paint, dust and grime he looked like he might be in danger of having a tidy tablecloth thrown over him too.

"So did you manage to find anything about epilepsy on the web?" Mum asked.

I'd given Mum and Dad an update on Rachel when I got home from the Shingles café not so long ago. (Er, except I'd missed out the bit about scrambling inside Joseph's house – I didn't think they'd be too chuffed about me wandering round a condemned building.)

"Yeah, quite a lot," I said, blowing on a steamy forkful of lasagne. "But you know something weird? Rachel said that since her first seizure, she can *sense* stuff."

I wasn't sure how this would go down with Mum and Dad. They're fun and laid-back and brilliant and everything, but they're not too good with "spook" stuff. Generally, they always come up with a "sensible" explanation. Or laugh. But right now, what Rachel had said had burrowed so much into my head that I couldn't keep it to myself.

"What kind of stuff?"

I quickly realized I couldn't mention the ghostly hide-and-seekers, 'cause then I'd have to admit to being in Joseph's house.

"Just figuring out what people are going to say before they say it, or what track's going to come on the radio next. That kind of thing."

"Well, it's probably not *exactly* like that," said Dad. "I bet Rachel's just feeling very highly strung and emotional at the moment, and is hyper-aware of everything going on around her."

I nodded at Dad, chewing too much to talk. I

wasn't sure if I was convinced by what he was saying, but it sounded a lot better than TJ's nutsville alien explanation (I'd have to check that boy's house for *Star Trek* and *X-Files* box sets. . .).

"The poor girl. She must be so scared – developing a condition like this out of the blue!" Mum sighed sympathetically. "And as for her friends being so unsupportive. . ."

"That's the bit I don't get!" I blurted out, now that I'd swallowed. "Why are Kayleigh and the others acting like that?"

"People are scared of things they don't understand," Dad said with a shrug. "Those girls are just immature and frightened. They don't know how to deal with something as grown-up as illness, so they just try to ignore it. It's their way of coping."

"But that's pathetic!"

"I know, Stella," Mum agreed, as she patiently took the fishfinger Jamie had chucked on to the table and put it back on his plate. "I remember my friend Lucy telling me about her older brother being killed in a motorbike accident when she was twelve. As if *that* wasn't hard enough to deal with, when she went back to school the following week, everyone ignored her."

"It wasn't because they were deliberately trying

to be horrible," said Dad, picking up the story (and the chucked fishfinger again). "In fact, I bet all her schoolfriends felt awful for her, but didn't know what on earth to say."

"But that's like you're making excuses for them!" I protested. "I mean, maybe that made *them* feel better, but it must have been miserable for Mum's friend!"

"I'm not trying to make excuses for people doing that, Stella, I'm just trying to explain why they were acting that way," said Dad, talking all super-sensibly, like the media lawyer he used to be back in London. "And I'm not making excuses for Rachel's friends either. I think maybe they just need some time to get used to the idea."

Yeah, but how long would that be? If *I* was Rachel, I don't think I'd have been in the mood for forgiving them, if they suddenly came grovelling to me a week or so down the line.

(Mind you, *I* was on the verge of forgiving Rachel, for all the bitchy looks and whispered digs her and her gang had thrown my way since I came to Portbay. . .)

"Oh, Stella – did I leave the pepper by the computer?" Dad suddenly asked. "I ate a sandwich through there at lunchtime when I was searching for DIY sites on septic tanks. . ."

"I'll go see," I offered, noticing that Dad's hands were full trying to restrain Jamie from throwing the entire contents of his plate – bean by bean – on to the flowery tablecloth.

As I wandered back through to the computer, I suddenly wished me and TJ had made some kind of arrangement to meet up with Rachel again. We weren't doing anything in particular tomorrow – I could have asked her to come around here, and shown her my den or something.

Why hadn't we swapped mobile numbers? Well, we didn't and that was that. I guess I'd just bump into her around town again sometime. . .

"Hey, Peaches – where's the pepper?" I asked, as a green pair of eyes blinked open.

With a lazy yawn, Peaches stretched out, putting his paw right on the pepper pot. And as his stretch turned into an arc, a section of the local paper suddenly became visible, now that it wasn't covered by hairy tummy any more.

An ad with the heading *The Portbay Galleria* leapt out at me in swirly, fancy writing. That was Rachel's mum's shop down on the prom; it sold lots of arty-crafty bits-and-bobs to tourists and specialized in terrible paintings of seaside scenes.

". . .*looking for contributions of local art for an*

exhibition to be shown during the upcoming Portbay Gala Week. Anyone interested should call Amanda Riley on. . ."

Amanda Riley, that must be Rachel's mum. There were two phone numbers printed there – one for the shop (daytime) and one for home (evenings).

"So . . . I could call this and ask to speak to Rachel, couldn't I?"

Peaches blinked his green eyes and yawned lazily again.

"D'you think I should give it a go?" I asked, a little voice in my head worrying that Rachel might not be worth the effort. Or maybe she would. Or maybe she wouldn't. Or maybe she would. Or maybe I'd go bananas trying to decide.

"Prrrrr. . ." prrrred Peaches.

Well, who could argue with that? Straight after tea, I'd give Rachel a call.

Keeping my fingers crossed behind my back that I wasn't making a terrible mistake. . .

CHAPTER 11

Impressing Rachel (not)

Even with a great big purple bruise on her cheek, Rachel was really, truly, amazingly pretty.

As she gazed around my den, it was all I could do to stop myself from staring at her. With those heavy-lidded almond eyes and her silky, dark-brown hair, she was the human equivalent of an elegant Burmese cat, or a really beautiful deer or something. In designer tracksuit bottoms, of course.

"What's that?"

"That's my cat, Peaches," I told Rachel, watching his Fat Furriness wind his way around her legs.

"Won't he shed hair on my clothes?" she asked worriedly.

"No," I lied, just fascinated to watch Peaches' response to her. He'd been the same with TJ. Even when I wasn't sure of someone, *he* seemed to be. And you've got to trust spooky ginger cats who are smarter than you, haven't you?

"Those photos; those were the ones you had in the café on Tuesday. . ." said Rachel, eyeing the handful of snaps that were lying out on my old wooden desk.

For a second me, TJ and Rachel were all silent; me and TJ remembering the nasty little comments we got from Rachel's gang about these same pictures. For Rachel, I guessed, it reminded her more about collapsing with all eyes on her.

Quickly, I scooped the Fake Fairy Photo Project into the Snappy Snaps envelope they came in and shoved them in the drawer. When I glanced back up, Rachel was noseying around at all the trinkets on my shelves.

"What's with the cruddy old button?" she asked, peering inside the wooden box on the second shelf up.

The tone of her voice made it sound like she thought I might be a freak who'd turn up on a reality TV show about people who hoarded rubbish for fun.

"You know the servant guy I told you about? The one who Joseph's house is named after?"

Rachel blinked her almond eyes blankly at me. I'd kind of planned on telling her who I thought she'd "sensed" yesterday in the big house, depending on how things went this morning. No point sharing all my secrets if she wasn't up for hearing them.

"Well, I think this button is from Joseph's coat!" I continued to explain, feeling my way with her. "I think Elize Grainger must have kept it as a memento of him. There's this big family portrait of Elize with her parents at Portbay Museum, and Joseph's in the background in a red servant's jacket with the exact same buttons!"

"Yeah?" said TJ, picking the button out of the box and flipping it round in his fingers.

How weird that neither TJ nor Rachel had the faintest idea of their home town's history.

"Haven't you ever been to the museum?" I asked them both.

"With school once," said TJ. "But all I remember about it is that Darren Appleby touched a windowsill that had a sign beside it saying 'Do not touch' and got white paint all over his hand."

"Yeah, I was on that school trip too," Rachel chipped in. "Do you remember they had that one cabinet just full of boring *stones*?!"

I had a feeling Rachel was talking about fossils, but it didn't seem worth mentioning.

"See this?" I said, holding up the ornately painted, rose-decorated cup and saucer that I'd found in the den when I'd been clearing it out.

Rachel blinked dubiously, probably wondering why I was holding up a piece of old crockery for her to examine.

"Well, check this out. . ."

Rachel squinted at the yellowed newspaper I was holding out for her to see. The date on it was some time in 1930, and there was Elize Grainger, celebrating her hundredth birthday in what was now our garden. On a table beside her was an easel with a half-finished painting of a flower fairy, and also a rose-decorated cup and saucer.

"So, it's the same mug thing," muttered Rachel, making the connection but not really getting as excited as I'd have liked.

Maybe TJ had been right.

When I'd phoned him last night and said I'd invited Rachel around, he'd warned me that feeling a bit sorry for Rachel was *one* thing, but trying to be all matey with her was something else (i.e. a *bad* something else).

After he'd said that, I'd felt a bit dumb for thinking that an innocent "prrrr. . ." from Peaches had meant anything except for "prrrr. . .". Why did I let a happy cat sigh influence me at all?

Because Rachel had sounded sort of pleased when I phoned her last night, that's why. A bit freaked out at first, yes; but then pleased. And what options did she have? Spending a lovely, sunny, summer holiday day mooching about in her house on her own?

She hadn't come on her own just now though – her mum had dropped her off, looking like a blur of waving hands as she sped off to open the Portbay Galleria late.

"She doesn't trust me not to have a seizure," Rachel had sighed when she arrived ten minutes ago. "She says I can stay as long as I like, but I've got to give her a phone when I want to leave, and she'll come collect me."

You could tell Rachel hated the idea of being supervised. I guess that's the benefit of living in a small town, and normally wandering your days away with three other friends. As long as you're all together and all looking out for each other, it's like you've got your own protective pack. Only now Rachel wasn't a hundred per cent well, AND she didn't have a pack any more. . .

"And what's that?"

Now Rachel was staring at the one and only photo of my mum's mum and my grandad Eddie.

Meanwhile, TJ was still playing around with the brass button in his fingers, mesmerized by the thought of a ten-year-old boy – brought all the way over from Barbados – landing in England and being expected to be someone's servant. Outside, Ellie was randomly sticking buttercups from the garden into Bob's thick, long fur, as he panted happily and patiently. (Luckily, Jake and Jamie were having their nap at the moment, or no one – human or canine – would've been looking so relaxed.)

I suddenly wished I was just alone with TJ, or out sticking buttercups in Bob's fur, instead of looking after this girl who didn't want to be looked after.

And the last thing I wanted to do was try and explain why I only had one photo of my nana Jones and Grandad Eddie together. If I told Rachel that they'd dated when they were very young, and split up before either of them knew Nana Jones was expecting my mum, then in Rachel's perfect world that would sound seedy. And it wasn't. It was true love that got thwarted (great word that means "split up", sort of) because Nana Jones's parents didn't approve of Grandad Eddie being black.

"That's my mum's parents, when they first started dating," I explained, trying to sound casual as I stared at the photo of two teenagers in love, with the backdrop of the fair that Grandad Eddie worked on behind them both.

"Right. . ." said Rachel, staring some more but sounding unimpressed.

I felt too sensitive about that photo. I needed to get her to put it down now.

"They're both dead," I said bluntly, taking the framed picture from her and returning it to its place on the shelf.

"*He's* not."

"Excuse me?" I blinked at Rachel. Nana Jones had died a long, long time ago, that I knew for sure. And my mum had often said that the chances were that Grandad Eddie was dead too, since no one had ever known what became of him.

"Uh . . . sorry," Rachel lisped more heavily than usual on the "s". She seemed confused and bemused, as if she'd aimed to pick up a glass of milk and ended up sipping whatever stagnant water was in the flower vase.

TJ stared hard at me, same as he had yesterday in Joseph's house, when Rachel had come out with that whole ghostly hide 'n' seek thing.

"I have no idea why I just said that," murmured Rachel, still staring at the photo.

Neither did I. All I knew was that the hairs on my arms were standing on end, like it was a frosty morning in November instead of a baking hot lunchtime in early August.

"Can we do something else now?" Rachel asked suddenly, looking confused and embarrassed and in desperate need to get out of the den.

"Um . . . actually, we could watch *this*, if you fancy!"

As he spoke, TJ bent down and pulled a video out of a plastic bag he'd brought with him.

"What is it?" I asked, reaching out to take the tape and read the title scribbled in biro on the side of it.

"Aha! You'll have to wait and see!" TJ teased, hiding the tape behind his back. . .

I think Rachel was hoping for something cool, like a *Scream*-type horror movie or maybe an American High School tale of glam cheerleaders dating cute college baseball stars.

"It's about *fairies*?!" said Rachel, crinkling her tiny nose in disgust as the opening credits burst on the screen. "Isn't it for kids or something?"

She was staring hard at TJ, who went pink in the face as he pressed the volume button on my TV's remote.

"Hey, this is the story of the girls who faked the original fairy photos – like the ones me and Stella did!" he explained, trying to justify his choice of film. (He'd come across it at the back of his TV cabinet, when he'd been looking for a blank video to tape an episode of *Robot Wars* or something equally loud, dumb and boy-ish.)

"And TJ's mum acts in it too!" I told Rachel.

She narrowed her eyes and did one of those dismissive neck slide things that girls always do in hip-hop videos on MTV. I didn't suppose her and Brooke and Kayleigh and Hazel often watched many heart-warming, family-entertainment movies together.

"We can fast-forward through it if it's rubbish." TJ shrugged, looking kind of irked and discouraged at Rachel dissing the movie before it had even begun.

"Shush!" hissed Ellie, turning round from her lounging position directly in front of the TV, her blonde hair entangled with Bob's browny-black fur as she used his back as a cushion for her head.

And so we shushed, and didn't even fast-forward, since the film never turned out to be rubbish. It was pretty good, with special effect fairies flitting in and out, so you never knew if the girls (two cousins) had made the whole thing up or not. Just after the final scene – when the soldier dad of one of the cousins turns up after being missing, presumed dead, Ellie asked a very pertinent question.

"Where was Mum?"

"Dunno," said TJ, who'd got so caught up in the story that he'd forgotten that was one of the reasons we were supposed to be watching the film in the first place. "Maybe her scene got cut, or maybe she was so far in the background that we didn't recognize her."

I turned to Rachel, to see if she'd fallen asleep at the general un-coolness of it all.

But she wasn't asleep. She was crying.

"I'm OK! OK?" she said hurriedly, dabbing at her eyes and blowing her nose.

Ah, how sweet – Princess Trendy had a squishy soft centre. And anyone who can go mushy at a soppy movie can't be all bad, right?

"AAAAAAAAAAAAAAAARRRGHHH!"

"BOOOOOBBBBBBBB!"

Rachel's mushy mood turned to one of horror as my two little brothers hurtled into the room like thigh-high hurricanes and aimed themselves directly at TJ's rudely awakened pooch.

"Er, fancy going for a walk or something?" Rachel suggested.

She probably meant *without* my brothers, I guessed.

"Sure," I said, as TJ darted past the tangle of dog and kids and rescued his tape from our player. "Where do you fancy?"

"Aha! You'll just have to wait and see!" replied Rachel, nicking TJ's line from earlier.

She'd stopped crying, and looked more like her usual self. In fact, tossing her long dark hair back, Rachel suddenly looked a lot more like the conceited, cocky girl she used to be when she hung out with Kayleigh and co. And I wasn't sure I liked that.

At *all*. . .

The sin of slagging Bob

"Isn't this *bad* for epileptics?" TJ whispered to me, as Rachel bobbed and weaved in her seat, the virtual sci-fi sports car on the pixelating digital screen in front of her careering and crashing through imaginary neon streets.

Apparently, TJ didn't whisper quietly enough.

"Look, until I get the results of my hospital tests, I don't know if I *am* epileptic – OK?" Rachel answered defiantly, racking up the score as she avoided obstacle after obstacle.

"Um, weren't you meant to phone your mum?"

That was me, panicking quietly that Rachel's idea of "a little walk" had taken me, her and TJ all the way from my little house high up on a back street of town down to the Fun Arcade on the prom.

Me and TJ had thought we'd only be gone five or ten minutes, which is why we'd left Ellie and Bob at my place, happily buttercupping in the garden, with Jake and Jamie joining in this time round. But it had been a whole half-hour now, and Rachel didn't look like she was planning on heading home any time soon.

"I'm supposed to phone my mum when I want a lift. *That* was the deal," said Rachel, as firmly as anyone could with a lispy, little-girl voice.

She clamped her jaws tightly together as she leant into a particularly tight corner on the screen.

"And I *don't* want to go home yet," she added, narrowly avoiding a school bus of kids and a stray robot cat in the road ahead of her.

Rachel's mum was only about nine or ten shops away. We didn't know Mrs Riley, but we had a feeling that she'd probably *kill* me and TJ if she thought we weren't looking after her little girl properly. Still, I was almost willing to take that chance: if either me or TJ zipped along the prom and caught up with her mum now, Rachel would be back under armed guard in about five minutes, and me and TJ could relax.

"Listen, Rach," said TJ, a vein standing to attention in his neck, I noticed. "I've got to get back to Stella's house; I can't leave Stella's parents looking after my sister and my dog!"

"That dog!" Rachel suddenly giggled, her hand

still wedged on to the shiny silver steering wheel in front of her. "God, that dog of yours is like a smelly old blanket, isn't it?!"

Uh-oh.

Slagging off Bob in front of TJ was just about the most *awful* sin you could ever commit. It was like saying Ellie was noisy and annoying at times, which she was. Just like Bob really *did* smell like a smelly old blanket in hot weather. But you didn't just come out and say stuff like that, did you? It really was the way TJ had tried to explain to me the other day. . . Rachel and her mates didn't live in the real world: they thought they had a God-given right to say whatever *ping*ed into their selfish minds, and it didn't even dawn on them that they might hurt someone.

Screechhhhhhhh. . .! BANG! Doodly-oodly-ooodly OOO. . .!!

OK, it looked like Rachel had crashed and the game was over. Maybe we could all go home (one way or another) and forget this day had ever happened.

"Lend us another pound!" Rachel suddenly begged TJ. "Go on!"

"Nah," TJ shrugged uncomfortably. "I've got to get back. . ."

"C'mon, Beanie Boy! I only asked for a pound!"

Poor TJ's face froze, and for once, I did his talking for him.

"He hasn't got any money," I told Rachel, though I wasn't technically sure if that was true or not. What I *did* know was that I was about to lie for myself. "And neither do I. So maybe we should all go home now. . ."

All thoughts of that weird comment she came out with when she'd stared at my grandad Eddie's photo were gone. And all warm fuzzy feelings after watching the fairy film together were gone too. I just needed to get this ungrateful, casually cruel girl out of my sight. And fast.

"Whatever," Rachel squeaked glumly, slipping out of the looky-likey sports car. "Just one thing, though. . ."

I wasn't in the mood for "one thing, though". I was in the mood to go back home and spend the afternoon hanging out with TJ and his smelly blanket of a dog in the garden, maybe painting ninja fairies, or maybe watching Ellie boss my brothers about or vice versa.

"What?" I asked, feeling a little cagey.

Rachel's almond eyes blinked fast at me, a flurry of worry obvious from her expression.

"Can you guys walk me to my mum's shop, just

in case, y'know, whatever happens?"

Urgh. Now I felt bad again, remembering how ill Rachel could possibly be. TJ glared at her, then me, then rolled his eyes.

"Sure," I nodded, answering for both of us and letting TJ lead the way towards the door of the Fun Arcade.

"Oh, and something else, Stella. . ."

Rachel was hanging back a bit, letting TJ slip out of view and out of earshot. Her normally cool and confident almond eyes looked rounder and more appealingly at me.

"Stella . . . I've got to go for these tests at the hospital tomorrow afternoon. Can you come with me?"

Ker-BLAM.

That was the sound of all the last half-hour's bad feelings slipping away.

"Of course," I told her, feeling touched that she'd asked me.

Not to mention horribly horrible because I'd wanted to run away from her very fast a mere nano-second ago. . .

"Check out that seagull," said Dad wistfully, pointing to the bird lazily circling above us. "Now *that's* freedom!"

"Dad, it's after our chips," I told him bluntly, knowing a greedy, cross-eyed, psycho seagull when I saw one.

It was six o'clock, Thursday evening.

If we'd been back in our flat in London, this is what'd be happening: Dad would just be finishing work, and wouldn't be home for another hour yet; Mum would be giving the boys their tea, and would be a bit grumpy with tiredness; I'd be eating my tea in front of MTV, escaping from my brothers for a little bit till I had to help Mum bathe them and put them to bed.

But me, Mum and Dad and the twins; we weren't in London, we were in Portbay. And we were having fish and chips on the beach, in the early evening sunshine, just because we could, and it was a lovely thing to do. (Also, Dad had banged a stepladder against the gas cooker and knocked two of the control knobs off and Mum was refusing to use it till the repair guy had been.)

Me, Mum, Dad and the twins . . . all parked on mismatching, overlapping towels, looking like a happy mismatching family, even though we were all well and truly related.

My goldy-brown curls were bouncing and

dancing around my face in the evening breeze, while Dad's short, white blond back and sides stayed just where it was meant to be. Mum's straight, dark brown hair was pulled back into an obedient stubby ponytail, leaving her a clear view of both my brothers. Not that Jamie needed much watching; he was sleepily sucking on a chip in his half of the double buggy, one hand fiddling with his strawberry-blond locks as he struggled to keep awake. Only Jake was still bouncing, kicking sand between his chubby bare toes as he bit into yet another chunk of battered haddock.

"So, Stella, are you all right about going with Rachel to the hospital tomorrow?" Mum asked, helping herself to another onion ring from the Styrofoam carton.

"I *think* so," I said, not sure how I was really feeling. I changed my mind about Rachel every ten minutes. *And* I wasn't really sure if it was going to happen – me going along with her to the hospital, I mean. After all, I didn't think Rachel had run the idea past her mother, and I hadn't a clue whether Mrs Riley would think it was a wonderful or stupid idea. I don't think I could have given a very good impression of myself to her earlier; all she saw of me (and TJ) was a blur as we ran away, after taking Rachel to the Galleria door.

"Well, I think it's a lovely thing you offered to do," said Mum, smiling encouragingly at me.

Er, technically, I hadn't really offered . . . Rachel had guilt-tripped me into it.

"And I'll phone Rachel's mother tomorrow at her shop just to confirm it's OK," she carried on.

Speaking of guilt, I knew Mum (and Dad) were just excited that I might make another friend in Portbay and were doing *everything* they could to encourage it, including explaining away Rachel's weird behaviour this afternoon.

"I bet she was just acting recklessly because she's rebelling against the idea that she might be ill," Dad had said when I told him about our non-fun trip to the Fun Arcade.

"Or embarrassed that you saw her soft side, when she was crying at the end of the movie," Mum suggested.

Thing is, Mum and Dad had to drag me here to Portbay kicking and screaming (OK, moaning and sulking). And they still seemed to feel pretty guilty about it. So much so, that I think if I'd said I was hanging out with the town's resident vampire, they'd make excuses for him too: "Likes to drink people's blood? It's probably just a phase

121

he's going through. Why don't you invite him for tea?"

Well, seeing as Mum and Dad were so keen on Rachel, I thought I might as well drop in that strange thing she'd said in the den. Let's see how they'd explain *that*!

"Mum. . . Rachel saw the photo of Nana Jones and Grandad Eddie today."

"Oh, yes?" said Mum, half-listening and half-concentrating on wiping smears of tomato sauce off Jamie's face now he'd nodded off.

"I told her who they were, and said they were dead. But Rachel pointed to Grandad Eddie and said, '*He's* not!'"

I waited, expecting to hear my dad launch into something about heightened emotions and over-sensitivity and it-all-meaning-nothing, but instead he said nothing, just gazed at Mum. Who was looking sad all of a sudden.

"Well, maybe she's right and maybe she's not," Mum said, trying to force a smile on her face and seem her normal bright self. "But there's no way we'll ever know, is there?"

Urgh.

Everything to do with Rachel this week had been a bit of a hassle, and now in a roundabout way, she'd helped me upset my mum.

122

It was definitely starting to look like TJ was right – being matey with Rachel *wasn't* such a good idea.

Maybe I could ask Mum to write me a sick note to get out of going to the hospital with her tomorrow. . .

CHAPTER 13

Waiting (im)patiently

Zero marks for effort. Minus ten for lack of imagination. That's how I'd score the long-ago person who came up with the names of the towns and places round here.

I mean, "Portbay", "Sugar Bay", "Rock Bay", "Castlebay", "Westbay" . . . can you see a (dull) theme going on there? I was in Westbay now, the bigger town just along from Portbay. It was – what's that word Auntie V likes to use? Oh, yes – more *cosmopolitan* than my new home town. It had a shopping centre, a six-screen cinema, two Indian restaurants and a hospital.

Westbay Hospital, that was its unimaginative name, and that's where I was currently dying of boredom. (Somebody get a doctor, quick!) I hadn't got Mum to write me a sick note after all, in fact, by the time I got up from a long lazy lie-in, Mum had already phoned Mrs Riley, got instantly chummy with her and arranged for me to be picked up at twelve.

It was now two o'clock and I was in the most dreary waiting room in the world, where there was a choice of exactly three things to read: a curly-edged copy of *Take a Break* magazine (dated 1998), a copy of the *Nursing Times* and the ingredients on the side of the carton of Ribena in my hand.

Out of sheer boredom and desperation, I'd read *Take a Break* from cover to cover, and now I knew many useful tips, including how to keep slugs off your polyanthus (use vinegar) and what to do when you run out of window cleaner (scatter cat litter). Or maybe it was the other way round. . .

After that, I'd moved on to *Nursing Times*, but felt sick when I came across a feature on bed sores and was too scared to flick any further in case there were any more gross photos lurking amongst its pages.

So now it was the turn of the carton.

. . .*Glucose, Fructose Syrup, Sucrose*. . . I read in my head, wishing I hadn't come today, or that Rachel and her mum could have just dropped me at the very impressive-looking shopping centre in the middle of Westbay, and they could have picked me up later, when all the tests were finished. We were supposed to be going for a pizza there afterwards anyway, so I could've happily just bumbled round Miss Selfridge and HMV and the bookshops or whatever.

I didn't *mean* to sound mean when I said that, it's just that I'd been hanging around in this boring, claustrophobically small waiting room for nearly an hour and a half now, and I hadn't seen Rachel and her mum in all that time, not since a nurse came and swooped them away.

Since then, other people had come and gone and come again, occasionally whisked off along strange, shiny corridors to who knows where. None of them talked, not even to the people who'd come along with them. I didn't really know too much about hospitals . . . the last time I'd been in one was when the boys were born, but that ward was nuts and noisy with screaming babies, whereas this waiting room was deadly silent. Maybe there was a sign saying "Be Quiet!" somewhere among the posters about helplines and diseases I'd never heard of.

A sign I'd really have liked to have seen was for the ladies' loos – one carton of Ribena on and I was starting to get desperate. But I was too shy to ask the hassled-looking receptionist behind the glass partition where it was, knowing that in front of all these silent adults in this silent room, my thirteen-year-old voice would shake and stammer for all it was worth. I mean, it's bad enough stammering in general, and a *hundred* times as bad if you're asking where the t-t-t-t-toilet is while everyone's listening. . .

. . .*Citric Acid, Water, Vitamin C*. . . I read some more, trying to take my mind off the boredom and my bladder.

Meanwhile, the non-reading part of my brain started ticking over with daft thoughts – what if someone was playing a huge, involved practical joke on me? What if Rachel had faked her fits all along? What if her and her mum had been led along a corridor to the "out" door and were now having coffee, cake and a giggle at my expense back at Shingles café? What if there were half a dozen hidden TV cameras pointed on me now, picking up on my lips moving as I read out the contents of my Ribena carton? The whole of Britain would watch me, thinking I was nutty as a packet of dry roast.

And I *was* nuts, for coming up with stuff like that. Maybe *I* should be the one asking for the brain scans, and not Rachel. Or maybe I just needed to get out of here. . .

"Ah, Stella!" came a sudden voice, as Rachel's mum breezed into the waiting room and woke everyone up with her confident, don't-care-who's-listening voice.

Mrs Riley had steely grey hair cut into a hip style and wore casual clothes that looked expensive. I was quite intimidated by her, but I kind of liked her. She made life easy when you were shy (like I was) by talking all the time and answering her own questions. ("What was it like for you, leaving London? Must have been difficult"; "Are your brothers little terrors? They must be if they're at the 'terrible twos'. . .") Mrs Riley's non-stop chatarama had been brilliant in the car here, mainly 'cause Rachel had said nothing at all, just stared listlessly out of the car window.

"Rachel will be along in a second," her mum announced, settling herself down beside me. "She's had her ECMRGX%* scan now, and she's just nipped to the loo."

Mrs Riley didn't *really* say ECMRGX%*. I'd just got a bit muddled at all the possible EEG, MRI, X-ray and whatever else tests Rachel's mum had mentioned during the drive over.

Still, the important thing was that Mrs Riley knew where the toilet was. I was about to ask her when she slipped her hand over mine and looked (uncomfortably) deep into my eyes.

"While we're on our own, Stella, I just wanted to say something."

The other four people in the waiting room held their breath and leant forward ever so slightly, so they could hear better, I was sure.

"I'm *so* grateful to you for everything you've done this week. I know you helped pull Rachel out of the swimming pool, and myself and her father can't thank you enough for that."

"OK," I said, in a tiny, embarrassed squeak. I could feel four sets of eyes boring into me – make that five now that the receptionist had paused in her busy-ness to earwig.

It was also nice to be thanked. It meant Rachel had at least told her parents what me and TJ had done, even if she hadn't got around to thanking us – let alone *mentioning* it to us – herself.

"And you know, I've been *so* disappointed in her other friends. None of them have called or come round – not one! It's terribly up-setting for Rachel on top of all this and I know having you come with her today means an awful lot."

See? There I went again, changing my mind about Rachel in the flicker of an eye. One second

I was grumpy with her for acting ungrateful, and the next, I was achingly sorry for her.

And how could I whinge to myself about needing the loo and only having bedsores and slugs to read about when poor Rachel had been poked and prodded around for the last hour and a half?

"You know, I have to say, I've never been entirely happy with her hanging around with those girls," Mrs Riley admitted, in a loud, conspiratorial whisper. "Especially that Kayleigh girl. Our Rachel's changed a lot since she's been friends with them."

Ooh . . . *that* was an interesting thing to hear. It kind of helped answer the question I had about Rachel, i.e. deep down, was she a nice girl who'd just been influenced by Kayleigh? (Or deep down, was she as bitchy and shallow as Kayleigh?)

I was hoping Mrs Riley would tell me more – even though blasting off about her daughter's private life in her very loud voice in a very public place probably wasn't the most fantastic idea in the world. But Mrs Riley bounced on to the topic of Rachel's condition instead. Which, considering what she had to say next, *also* wasn't the most fantastic idea in the world.

"Ah, my poor little Rachel!" she sighed, tilting her head to one side as she gazed my way. "How could we have guessed she'd develop epilepsy?"

"So . . . it *is* definitely epilepsy, then?" I asked.

"The doctors are ninety-five per cent sure, but we'll have to wait till all the results of all the tests are back. But they can never be sure of why she might have developed it. They ran through a few possible reasons, but none of them fitted in Rachel's case."

"What sort of reasons?" I quizzed Mrs Riley, vaguely remembering reading something about this on the internet site I'd found.

"Well, it can sometimes be as the result of a head injury, or if you were prone to fits as a baby," she said. "And sometimes teenage girls can develop it around the time of puberty. But that doesn't fit in Rachel's case – she started her period *well* over a year ago and—"

"*Mum!*" gasped a sharp voice from the waiting room doorway, making all of us jump, and sending a last dribble of Ribena squishing out of the carton on to my light denim mini-skirt.

The person doing the gasping was Rachel and she was staring straight at her mum, a look of anger and embarrassment slapped across her face.

"What?" Mrs Riley said in surprise. "I was just explaining to Stella what the doctor said!"

Yeah, well, maybe . . . but I guess having a waiting room full of people knowing when you started your period was pretty mortifying.

"In front of *everyone*?!" Rachel hissed, dropping her head down enough to let her hair fall forward and shield her burning cheeks a little.

"Oh, don't be so dramatic, darling!" Mrs Riley said pleasantly, standing up now and getting ready to leave. "Now, when did they say to make another appointment?"

I couldn't believe Mrs Riley was being so insensitive.

"How do *I* know?" grouched Rachel, turning side on in the doorway and looking like she might be about to do a runner.

"Well, can you remember when the doctor said the results would be back?"

"*I* can't remember, *can* I!"

"There's no need for that tone, darling – I just couldn't remember if it was two or three weeks, and I was only asking a quest—"

"Oh, just *shut* up, Mum! Just *shut* up! OK?"

"Well, I suppose I'd better just check with the receptionist," said Mrs Riley, casting a puzzled glance at her daughter.

The receptionist, I noticed, instantly tried to look casually professional, as if she *hadn't* just been listening to everything that was going on.

I tried to look casual (if not professional), and began idly reading the contents list on the carton again. The one thing I couldn't do was look Rachel in the eye after that little outburst. Her mum might have been a bit insensitive, blabbing all that stuff, but how could Rachel talk to her like that? I'd *never* speak that way to Mum in a million years! I wasn't ever that horrible and snappy even when she told me – along with Dad – that we were moving and it felt like the end of my little world. . . And how come Rachel's mum was letting her get away with it? Was it just 'cause she'd been through a whole heap of horrible tests? I had a funny feeling it wasn't just that.

And then it dawned on me – maybe Rachel was just plain, old-fashioned *spoilt*.

I'd never been friends with anyone like that before and I didn't see why I should start now.

Except that I just sneaked a peek at Rachel and spotted a fat tear rolling down her bruised cheek as she struggled to hold her defiant expression.

OK, so now I felt sorry for her again.

Nurse – help! I have a severe case of confusion of the brain, caused by close contact with Rachel Riley. . .

CHAPTER 14

Three sorrys and a curious

"They think he's dead," I said to TJ, staring across several tables and clocking a couple leaning over Bob's flopped, hairy body on the pavement outside. "Should we go and tell them he's OK?"

We weren't sitting at the window seat of the Shingles café today, and so weren't in knocking distance of the glass.

"Nah, he'll start snoring soon and they'll know he's all right," said TJ, concentrating on the three white sugar lumps he was juggling.

This time there was no Ellie with us (she'd gatecrashed her mother's Friday morning junior drama workshops). But there *was* Rachel (she'd been in the ladies' for a very, *very* long time now). TJ had suggested she might have accidentally flushed herself down the loo. When he comes out with stuff like that, you just have to ignore him. . .

"D'you think she's all right with us making her

come here?" he asked now, never taking his eyes off his mini, square, sweet-tasting juggling balls.

"Dunno," I shrugged, because I didn't. Know, I mean.

When Mrs Riley dropped me off after the hospital yesterday, Rachel had asked if we could hang out again today. I'd phoned TJ later to report on how the whole hospital thing had gone – missing out the part about her mum talking periods loudly ('cause I thought it might make him squirm) and the bit about Rachel yelling at her mum to shut up ('cause he'd probably think the worst of Rachel and refuse to hang out with her ever again). Anyway, when I asked if he had any suggestions about where we could meet up, the first thing he'd suggested was the Shingles café.

"She's not going to be up for that, though, is she? Not when she collapsed last time she was there!" I'd pointed out.

"Yeah, but that's exactly why she *should* go back."

At first, I thought TJ was just being plain *rotten*, but then he explained that the sooner Rachel got over what happened in the café, the better. It was like that old saying, the one that goes on about falling off horses or bikes or camels or whatever, and how important it is to get back on straightaway or you lose your nerve.

And let's face it, since the Shingles was the only decent café in town, Rachel didn't have much choice, unless she wanted to spend the rest of the summer holidays wandering the streets of Portbay with a Thermos flask and a packed lunchbox.

"By the way, have you found anything to like about her yet?" TJ asked, his eyes darting in looping circles as he followed the swirling sugar lumps.

I opened my mouth to protest and then realized I couldn't think of an answer straightaway. Oops.

"You're just sorry for her 'cause of her epilepsy, and 'cause she's got lousy friends, and 'cause she's got that slight lisp thing going on."

"It's not just that!"

"Oh, yeah? Ah, and of course, you're kind of curious about the psychic stuff she's been talking about. So basically, that's three sorrys and a curious, and that's not really the best start to a friendship!"

I'd have liked to have been able to say something smart and convincing in reply, but the *real* reason I kept giving Rachel chance after chance was that Peaches kept purring every time I mentioned her name. I couldn't *quite* see why he rated her so much, but I had to trust him, since he'd been right about TJ.

Not that I felt I could *tell* TJ that he'd become my mate because of a scruffy, fat, spook cat.

Still, I thought to myself, *I could mention a certain something to do with it. . .*

"TJ, I gave *you* a chance, even *after* you nicked my mobile off me. So you can't give me a hard time about giving Rachel a break!"

"But it was a dare! They made me!" TJ protested.

Of *course* I knew that Sam's gang had made him, and of *course* I knew how sorry he was about it, but I think it got my point across. He didn't *say* he got it though, 'cause Rachel finally came back and slithered into her seat.

In front of her was a giant chocolate, strawberry and vanilla ice-cream sundae that Phil the café owner had presented to her free, when we first came in. She'd only had about two mouthfuls, which was weird. Well, you *are* a weirdo if you turn down free ice cream, aren't you?

Rachel didn't even *look* at the melting, milkshaky mush it had turned into, let alone *eat* it. Maybe she'd gone off the idea now that she'd smeared half a pot of gloss on her lips. *And* the rest.

"What's all that stuff on your face?" TJ asked straight out, with typical boy-ish bluntness. I think he was quite enjoying this aspect of Rachel being our on-trial friend – he could talk to her straight rather than tiptoe around her like he felt he had to when she was in her little clique. Specially as she seemed to be on her best behaviour today. Was this the real Rachel, and not the spoilt, I'll-do-what-I-want-when-I-want girl we'd seen so much of? I hoped so.

"I decided to put on some make-up to hide my bruise," said Rachel, lightly touching her cheek. "Didn't want anyone staring and feeling sorry for me."

The toe of a Converse trainer collided with my shin. Thanks, TJ – I got the message. Rachel didn't like people feeling sorry for her. Specially not three-times-sorry, I didn't suppose.

"So what did the doctors at the hospital – *oops* – say to you yesterday, Rach?" asked TJ, dropping his sugar lumps in mid-juggle as I tapped him lightly on the shins back. "Is it definitely epilepsy that you've got?"

Ooh, don't go there, I thought to myself, reliving

the horrible tension in the car on the way back from Westbay. Mrs Riley couldn't understand why Rachel had said she wasn't up for the treat of going for a pizza, and as she babbled on, Rachel said nothing – just stared out of the car window under her curtain of dark hair. (Fun for me – not. Though all I could think about was that fat tear sliding down Rachel's bruised cheek in the waiting room doorway. . .)

"Probably," Rachel sighed in reply to TJ's question, as she stared vaguely in the direction of the window. Where a little old lady was currently standing laughing at Bob's snores.

A little old lady in a pink netting hat and green raincoat.

I waved at Mrs Sticky Toffee, and was about to point her out to the others when she abruptly wandered off. And anyway, Rachel was in mid-explanation. Since she was talking about something so heavy, I didn't really want to interrupt her to say, "Hey, *there's* the old lady who gives me toffees sometimes!" It didn't seem quite right. . .

"Anyway, I've got to go back when they get the test results in and then they'll tell me for sure if it's epilepsy, and what type it is, 'cause there're loads. If it is – and it probably is – I might have to take drugs every day for the rest of my *life*."

"Wow. . . So did they say how you could've caught it?" TJ asked, scrabbling around the table for his looky-likey juggling balls.

Ooh, *really* don't go there, TJ. . .

"You don't *catch* epilepsy," snapped Rachel. "It's a condition that just *happens*."

She sounded instantly tetchy, obviously thinking of the scene with her mother in the waiting room too.

"Well, how come it just happened to *you*, then?" TJ persisted.

"Don't know, the doctor didn't say," shrugged Rachel, trying to sound casual, even though I could tell her face had flushed pink, even *under* her layer of make-up.

As she spoke, she shoved her tall glass of melted sundae away from her.

Suddenly I wondered something . . . could it have anything to do with *food*, maybe? Maybe Rachel didn't eat enough. She was about the same shape as the spoon by the side of the tall glass after all, i.e. slim to the point of skinny. Could *that* have anything to do with her epilepsy? Not knowing her well enough, it didn't seem like the sort of question I could ask her. ("Hey, are you, like, borderline anorexic or something?")

Maybe I'd look up that epilepsy site on the internet later on when I got –

She'd gone weird.

It took TJ only a split-second longer than me to spot it too. It wasn't seizure weird, it was spaced-out-'cause-I've-sensed-something weird.

"Rach, what is it?" I asked, putting my hand on one of hers and being surprised at how cold it was.

"They're coming . . . they're all coming . . . and they're together!" she mumbled, her eyes fixed on the plate-glass window at the front of the café and the empty pavement beyond.

We didn't have long to wait to see what she meant – both me and TJ had only just turned our heads when a bundle of boys and girls cast a shadow over the large room, right before their laughter and chatter burst inside.

Kayleigh, Brooke and Hazel; Sam, Aiden, Ben and Marcus. Both gangs (queen bee girls, baddish boys) had always vaguely flirted with each other, from what I'd seen of them. But it stunned me to see them all acting *quite* as cosy – specially when everyone on Tuesday had heard Sam's lot cackling as Rachel fainted away and trembled through her seizure.

Course, I wasn't the person who was most surprised. Rachel's mouth hung slightly open, her bottom lip trembling in disbelief.

If she'd thought *that* was bad, it was about to get a whole lot worse. . .

"Hey, Rach! How you doing?!" Sam called out, sounding at first amiable, then stopping and doing a shuddering, cross-eyed, tongue-lolling, *mean* impersonation of her.

"Yeah, are you *thure* you're OK? 'Cauth we were *tho* worried about you!" sniggered Aiden, putting on a horribly exaggerated fake lisp.

Poor Rachel. Once upon a time (i.e. before her first seizure at the lido on Monday), she was the queen of the queen bees, impossibly pretty, lusted after by Sam and co, her tiny hint-of-a-lisp ignored or seen as cute. But now that she was imperfect, her glam girlfriends had turned their nasty little backs on her, and Sam and the other lads felt free to let rip with the insults and teasing.

"Ignore them, Rach," growled TJ protectively, having suffered years of insults and teasing himself. "Just act like they're not here and talk to us and it'll be –"

I guess he was going to say OK. But Rachel wasn't in the mood to wait around to hear it. She dashed for the door as fast as her posh trainers would take her, and it was a total trauma for me and TJ, trying to figure out how to go after her while searching our pockets for the money to pay for our drinks first.

Phil the owner made it easy for us.

"Square up later, guys – go get her," he ordered us with a wave of his huge muscular arm.

As I grabbed Rachel's bag and bolted, I flashed a grateful grin Phil's way, but he missed it – he was too busy glowering at the gloating crowd of boys and girls settling themselves at the café's biggest table. Phil was a businessman – I couldn't see him barring Sam and Kayleigh and the others when they were so keen to spend their money here. Still, if *I* was them I might worry that my burger had been deliberately *sneezed* on from now on.

"*Bark! Bark! Bark! Bark! Bark!*"

As far as I was aware, Bob was a long-haired Alsatian. But out on the pavement of the prom, overlooking the denim-blue sea and the sky-blue sky, he seemed to have channelled some long-forgotten sheepdog ancestor and started rounding up Rachel, whirling so many circles around her that she couldn't speed too far away from us.

"Rach! Hold on!" TJ urged, getting to her before me.

He looked up at her, but she'd covered her face with her hands.

"Good dog! There, there!" I quietened Bob, in case he was stressing Rachel any more than she was already stressed.

Bob eased off straightaway, giving me a haven't-I-been-a-good-boy? doggy grin and smelling of an odd mixture of old blanket and toffee. . .

I looked up in time to see Rachel slide her hands down her face, streaking the make-up off and leaving stripes where you could plainly see the hidden bruise on her left cheek.

"It's OK!" I blurted out, trying to hug her.

"It's *not* OK!" Rachel said back. "I feel like a freak! I have a freaky condition, which makes me look and act freaky, and my best mates have gone freaky on me!"

I struggled to think of something positive to say, to think of something calming. But the only image that came into my head was a fat, ginger cat purring noisily.

"You've got that psychic thing going on!" I reminded her. "Loads of people would love to have some kind of gift like that!"

"But I don't want it! I just want everything to be the way it *was*!"

To be honest, although I'd never willingly wish myself to have a condition like epilepsy, I couldn't exactly say that I understood Rachel wanting things back as they were. I mean, knowing now what heartless traitors her friends were, would she seriously want to zip back in time and hang out with drongos like them again?

"Rach – it's going to be OK," TJ tried to persuade her too.

"How?" sobbed Rachel, upsetting Bob enough to make him rumble a low "how-*ooooooo*!".

TJ shot a look my way, a look that yelled "Help!-I-don't-know-what-to-say!". But before I could come out with any useless waffle, he fixed his gaze somewhere over my head and started smiling. Seemed like he'd been hit by the inspiration stick.

"How?" he said to Rachel, gazing up into her tear-streaked face. "'Cause Madame Xara is going to sort everything out!!"

Who?! I mouthed at TJ, out of Rachel's eyeline.

TJ grinned like a boy-shaped Cheshire Cat and beckoned us both to follow him. . .

CHAPTER 15

I dare you to be spooked. . .

Madame Xara: Astral Reader, the sign outside the tiny shop on the prom read.

"I'm not going in *there*!" Rachel had squeaked. "She's just some dumb attraction for the tourists!"

"An 'astral reader'?" I frowned. "What's that — like a clairvoyant or something?"

"Guess so," said TJ. "I've never been in — don't know anyone who has."

"'Cause she's just for tourists, like I said!" Rachel insisted.

"Yeah, but what if she *can* see into people's futures?" TJ pointed out. "Maybe she'll be able to tell you what your life's going to be like, Rach. Maybe she'll tell you that everything's going to be OK, even if it feels like poo right now."

That was a nice thought on TJ's part, even if he'd come up with it in a moment of panic, while Rachel was flipping out. Not that she seemed to appreciate his efforts. . .

"No *way*!" Rachel muttered, staring at the shop front and shaking her head. "My mum says Madame Xara's probably an old fake, getting money off the holidaymakers for waffling some rubbish about moons in Uranus, or telling you your dead great granny says hello and she doesn't like your hair cut that way."

"Well, I guess your mum could be right. But what if this Madame Xara says something about all that stuff you've been sensing?" I suggested, with a ripple of excitement boinging around in my tummy. "Maybe she'll feel like you're a psychic, same as her!"

Rachel blinked her almond eyes silently for a second. Her face was still all streaky from where she'd rubbed her make-up off with her fingers or cried it down her cheeks.

"No – I'm still not doing it."

"But it could be dead good!" TJ tried to encourage her.

"Nope."

Rachel folded her hands across her chest and looked determined not to be persuaded. TJ almost looked like he was going to shrug and give up on the idea, when a glint came into his eye.

"*Dare* you!" he grinned.

"I said no!" Rachel replied, glowering at him.

"*Dare* you, you chicken!"

"I am *not* a chicken!"

I couldn't see how a stupid dare was going to convince her. TJ was wasting his time.

"*Wwwwwwuhhh.* . . Cluck! Cluck! Cluck!" he clucked, wafting his elbows up and down.

"Stop it!" Rachel ordered him.

TJ didn't stop. In fact, he kept up with the clucking and the elbow waggling, and added a hen-style strut into the bargain.

"TJ! I'm *not* a chicken, and I'm *not* going to do your stupid dare!"

"*Wwwwwwuhhh.* . . Cluck! Cluck! Cluck!" TJ clucked some more, winding up Rachel and confusing Bob.

"TJ O'Connell, you are the most annoying boy in the world!" Rachel growled.

That was it. She was going to stomp off in a huff any second now.

"*Wwwwwwuhhh.* . . Cluck! Cluck! Cluck!"

OK, so I know *nothing* about people. 'Cause five seconds later, a fuming Rachel went storming over to the net-curtained door of Madame Xara's shop.

"Dares – they work *every* time!" TJ muttered smugly to me, as we hurried after her. . .

*

"I don't usually like 'guests' being present at a reading," muttered the woman on the other side of the fancy lace tablecloth.

She was old-ish, but not *old* old. Her cream cardie was ancient, though, like it had been through a thousand washes and had the bobbles to prove it.

I was kind of fascinated by her make-up; she wore a lot of it, and the effect was like she'd splashed peach-coloured talc on her face instead of water this morning. The pearly, seashell-pink lipstick was a colour I'd never seen at any Boots beauty counter, and as for her sheeny-shiny blue eyeshadow, well, it matched her sheeny-shiny dangly blue earrings perfectly.

"Wooo-oooh! Scared yet?" TJ had whispered in my ear as Madame Xara led us from the waiting room (decked out drably like a dentist's) to her "parlour" (a back room with material pinned on the walls instead of paper, and a big table with a set of tarot cards placed on it).

I was quite scared – of her make-up – but I didn't get the chance to whisper that back before we were herded into our seats.

"Due to the private nature of what I might be about to unveil, I prefer to keep the sessions one-on-one," Madame Xara continued, pushing the

149

sleeves of her cardie up her podgy arms like she meant business. "But since you're just a young girl, Ruth –"

"Rachel," Rachel corrected her nervously.

"– *Rachel*, I'll make an exception."

Madame Xara had made an exception, all right. Instead of one client and one client only, she'd had to put up with *all* of us crushing in on her psychic session, i.e. Rachel, me, TJ and Bob.

Bob in particular seemed very excited by the stripes of nylony satin-look material on the walls and the overpowering smell of incense. He seemed to be panting and sniffing very hard, like he suspected a very exotic foreign dog might be hiding somewhere. If only he'd sit down and not look like he was about to lift his leg and spray everywhere. . .

"Here, boy, *SIT!*" TJ ordered his pet, as he spotted Madame Xara's eyes fix disapprovingly on Bob.

Doing as he was told, Bob huffed to a standstill, parking himself between the plastic waiting room chairs me and TJ had brought in, and thunking his shaggy head down on the table.

His nose was still active though. His nostrils flared and fluttered as they honed in on the smell of the incense and also the not-very-atmospheric waft of cheese. Next door was a shop called Cheese Please! (hey, guess what that sold), which must have been to blame for the pong, and the need for the incense as a cover up.

"OK, let's begin, then, Ru – I mean, Rachel. . ." said Madame Xara.

With a wary glance our way, Rachel took the pack of tarot cards from the woman's hand, and started shuffling them (badly) with shaky hands of her own.

Actually, I felt a little bit shaky too. What if Madame Xara suddenly turned to me, mumbling about a message coming through from my nana Jones? ("Helloooo, Stella! Sorry yoooo inherited my frecklessss!")

What if Nana Jones had a spooky message about my grandad Eddie? You know – something about him being alive and well and living in the Isle of Wight or something?

Under the table, my leg started drumming with excitement. Which made the two glass tealights on the table start tinkling together and earned me a "stop it!" look from Madame Xara.

"Now choose your first card, and put it *there*. . ." she told Rachel, turning her attention back to her client. "And choose another one and put it *there*. . ."

Rachel's face was taut with concentration as she slowly picked and laid out nine cards in a weird criss-cross pattern. Meanwhile, Madame Xara looked a little bored. Sitting as still and quiet as possible, I couldn't help notice the "astral reader" stifle a yawn, snatch a glance at her watch and scratch her long, permy, curls of vivid red hair. Which sort of moved. Not just the curls, I mean, but the *whole* thing. . .

Er, was it a *wig*?

"So. . ." Madame Xara intoned loudly, suddenly snapping into character and poring over the intricately decorated cards. "I see a lot of creativity here. . . Do you come from an artistic family?"

Rachel's face snapped from tight and tense to bright and bemused.

"Well, my dad's not really. . . But my mum runs the Portbay Galleria!"

"Hmmm, as I thought," Madame Xara mumbled under her breath. "And this card is telling me there's a tall, dark-haired boy in your life. He wears strange clothes, and there's something . . . something about his face . . . but I can't quite make it out."

"That'll be my brother, Simon! He wears black eyeliner *all* the time, and has about twenty of these awful, cruddy garage rock T-shirts," Rachel babbled at high speed. "And his lip's pierced – that's what you must be seeing!"

I wondered how it could be possible that everyone in the room wasn't staring at me and asking me what the thumping sound was. How could no one else hear the amplified POUND-POUND-POUND of my heart right now? TJ looked just as stunned by Madame Xara's accuracy. His lightly summer-suntanned face had gone pure white.

"Indeed, indeed," muttered Madame Xara with a knowing nod. "Ah, but now *this* one. . ."

"What's wrong with it?" Rachel asked, a frown flitting across her features, as Madame Xara tap-tapped a shimmery seashell-pink nail on a particular card.

"It's telling me you've not been very well lately, dear. Have you. . . Have you had an accident or a sudden illness perhaps?"

Wow.

Wow with sugar on top.

Madame Xara might have been a little on the grumpy side, had bad taste in make-up and strangely wobbly hair, but she sure was an ace astral reader. I couldn't *wait* to hear what she'd come up with next. . .

Knock, knock, knock!!!

For every knock, three people (and a dog) leapt in that little room. But not Madam Xara. Turning to a door behind her that I hadn't noticed before, she yelled, "I'm working, Henry! Go away!"

"But Mum!" a grown man's voice called out from the other side of the door. "I need to talk to you!"

Madame Xara took a deep breath and sighed, the shoulders of her cream cardie sinking.

"Excuse me for just one second," she told Rachel, as she got up from the table, disappeared out through the door and began a grouchy, whispered conversation with whoever was Henry. With the back door left open a crack, the breeze wafted in more of the cheddar-scented pong.

"Are you OK?" I asked Rachel, using the few moments to check on her.

"Yeah!" Rachel nodded enthusiastically. "She's really good, don't you think?"

"Definitely!"

"I mean, she got my family straightaway, and she knew about my epilepsy and everything!"

"I know!" I agreed, vaguely aware of TJ leaning across the table, like he was straining to hear what was going on outside.

"She hasn't mentioned anything about me sensing stuff yet, but she might, mightn't she?"

"Course!" I said, nodding hard. "Bet she'll get on to that next, before she starts on telling you your future and –"

With a firm thunk of the door, Madame Xara rejoined us, and TJ sat bolt upright.

"Rachel, I'm terribly sorry, but I'm going to have to draw this session to a close for today," she announced. "Something's come up. I won't charge you for this, and you're more than welcome to come back any time. I work mornings, and evenings at the weekend."

The four of us found ourselves being unceremoniously ushered towards the door, and a few seconds later we were out on the pavement in the glare of the midday sun.

"Oh. . . I *really* wanted to hear more!" Rachel grumbled with disappointment.

"*I* heard more!" TJ grinned at us both.

"Like what?" I asked him, wondering what he was finding so funny all of a sudden.

"Like the conversation Madame Xara was having with her son just now!"

"Which *was*?" Rachel frowned at TJ.

"Which was – him asking her if she was finished yet, 'cause a coach party had just arrived and he needed her to come and give him a hand."

"Give him a hand doing what?" I asked, feeling

pretty confused. I mean, what kind of help could a psychic give to a coach party?

"Check it out," said TJ, nudging his head to the left.

Me and Rachel turned our heads enough to see. . . What? Lots of tourists milling along the prom pavement, staring into shop windows (including Rachel's mum's place) and eating ice creams?

"There! *Look*!" TJ laughed, pointing to a line of little old ladies snaking out of Cheese Please!. "Doesn't that look like a coach party to you?"

I didn't get it. At all. And neither did Rachel. But TJ seemed to want to wander over and peer through the window, so like overly trusting sheep, we did the same.

"Bingo!"

When he glanced round at me and Rach and saw our obviously blank expressions, TJ's smile of glee faded a bit.

"Look who's just come scurrying through from the back, putting an apron on!" he said impatiently.

"So? It's some shop assistant. So what?" I frowned, finding myself examining a middle-aged woman with neatly cut, short grey hair, who was currently tying a white apron around herself.

She was probably about to put on one of those silly straw boaters next, same as the one the bloke serving was already wearing. In this weather, you'd get hot wearing one of those. And you would get really hot wearing that cream cardigan.

Cream cardigan. . .

Oh!

"See!" said TJ, grinning in my direction. "And check out her earring!"

I checked it out. The woman was wearing only one earring – a dangly sheeny-shiny blue one. She must have been in too much of a hurry when she changed out of her Madame Xara disguise, and only got as far as whipping off the curly auburn wig and one of the danglers.

"So. . . Madame Xara is also Mrs Cheese Please?"

"Exactly!" sniggered TJ.

I couldn't help sniggering myself after that. By morning (and evening at weekends), this woman was an astral reader, but during the busy periods, she was a cheesemonger. . .

"Hey, if she's so psychic," I grinned at TJ, "how come she didn't know the shop had got crowded and her son needed her to help serve?"

"Yeah!" said TJ, nodding madly. "And that must be how she knew the stuff about Rachel – she must have seen her and Si coming out of the Galleria, since it's only along the road! And I bet she heard about what happened in the café the other day!"

"*Well*," we both heard Rachel say suddenly. "Glad *you* two think it's so funny!"

She wasn't smiling. Unless there was a smile hiding underneath that scowl, but I doubted it.

"Um, that's 'cause it *is* funny, Rach!" TJ told her. "Not the part about what happened to you in the café the other day, I mean – just funny 'cause of Madame Xara being so cheesy!"

"But you made a fool of me! Is that funny *too*, Beanie Boy?"

Uh-oh. The obnoxious Rachel was well and truly back in town.

"*How* did I make a fool of you?" TJ frowned at her, clenching his teeth at the sound of that nickname.

"Making me believe a fake psychic, of course! What if anyone saw me coming out of there just now? I'd be *so* shamed!"

"We were only trying to cheer you up, Rach!" I tried to explain, wondering why I was bothering. "We didn't *know* she was fake. It was just a bit of fun, anyway. And who cares if anyone saw you?"

"That's all right for *you* to say, Stella!" Rachel

snapped back at me. "You're not *from* here. *I've* got a reputation in this town and—"

"Yeah, a reputation for being a spoilt, stuck-up, mean cow!"

That was TJ, striking a low (but fair) blow.

Just as if she'd been physically punched in the stomach, Rachel's mouth dropped open in surprise.

I bet in all her popular, pampered life, no one had *ever* spoken to her like that.

"Rach, you think you've got the right to do and say whatever you like, but you don't!" TJ blustered on. "We try and be nice to you, and you think it's OK to treat me and Stella like dirt. Well, meet the real world, Rachel! In the *real* world you've got to stop acting like a total baby and having hissy fits, and *think* before you open your big gob and let nasty little comments spill out!"

Rachel's face flushed angry red, making her mauve bruise glow deep purple on her cheek. She looked like she *might* be about to say something that involved X-rated words. But instead, she just turned and stormed off in the direction of her mum's shop.

"Spoilt git. . ." mumbled TJ, as he distractedly scratched Bob's hairy ears.

"Stella etc."; that was what my Auntie V said

when she was describing me and my friends back in London. When I got together with TJ, I thought it was the start of a whole new "etc." for me, here in Portbay.

Looked like moody old Rachel Riley wasn't going to be part of that "etc." any time soon. . .

ChapTeR 16

It's good to moan (and moan and moan)

When you're seriously hacked off with someone, it's like having a big, uncomfortable, twisted ball of metal in your chest.

The best thing you can do to get rid of that big, uncomfortable, twisted ball of metal is to have a moan. And after Rachel turned into a sulky little madam again yesterday, I really *did* need to moan.

I moaned to TJ after Rachel stormed off (and he moaned to me).

I moaned to Mum and Dad when I got home.

I moaned down the phone to Frankie last night.

I moaned to Neisha after I picked up an e-mail from her this morning.

In fact, the moan to Neisha was still ongoing.

Y'know, that Rachel sounds like a real

I didn't get to read the rest of this particular e-mail of Neisha's because Peaches sat on the keyboard and deleted it from my inbox.

"Thanks!"

"Prrrrrrrr. . ."

Now he started kneading the keys with his paws.

fkgorkhpOkj;i"]klo—%=';mjh

"Well, I'm not sure if that's a message you're trying to give me," I said, gently shoving Peaches off and reading the gibberish he'd "typed", "but I'm afraid I'm not fluent in spook-cat speak."

"Prrrrr. . ." purred Peaches, trying to make a cushion of my knees now.

"Maybe you didn't want to read anyone bad-mouthing Rachel, since you're such a fan of hers, eh?" I suggested, getting my shortish nails under Peaches' chin and giving him a good scratch.

"Prrrrrrrr. . ."

"One of us made a big mistake, didn't they, puss? Either *you* made a mistake thinking Rachel was OK, or *I* made a mistake thinking that's what you were trying to tell me!"

I was just about to e-mail Neisha again when an idea ambled into my mind.

"The fake fairy photos. . ." I muttered to

Peaches, as I stood up, lifting him in my arms like a sack of furry potatoes. "I could scan a couple of them in and e-mail them to Neisha and everyone!"

It would just be a bit of fun, and it wasn't as if me and TJ were going to do anything with them anyway. Might as well let *someone* see them, instead of just leaving them to gather dust in the drawer of my desk in the den.

Peaches kept up a vibrating purr as I carried him out into the garden. Cuddling a cat his size and weight wasn't easy, but I loved it, especially burying my nose into his scruffy gingerness and smelling his weird peaches'n'cream scent. Actually, he was almost as heavy as my brothers, who I attempted to cuddle sometimes too. The only problem with that was Jake tended to wriggle and Jamie tended to bite, and both of them whiffed of smelly nappies at close quarters. . .

"You're not really a small man in a cat-suit, are you?" I murmured to Peaches, as I practically staggered towards the den with him in my arms. "Or maybe an alien in a cat-suit, come to spy on humans and their inferior intelligence?!"

I was about to check his tummy for any sign of a zip or Velcro fastening when my mobile rang.

"It'll be TJ, seeing if I fancy doing something later," I told Peaches, by way of an apology as I put him down on the ground outside the den door. Not that he seemed to mind. The second his huge hairy feet hit the ground, he scampered off very speedily for a fat cat and leapt nimbly up on to the top of the back wall of the garden, which overlooked the alleyway.

"Hello?" I said vaguely, as I wrestled the latch free on the den door.

"Stella? It's Rachel. . ."

Oh. Wish we hadn't swapped numbers now – I didn't really fancy being snapped at again.

"Um . . . are you there, Stella?"

Rachel sounded two things – sheepish, and *near*.

"Yeah . . . hi," I replied flatly, not sure what to make of this.

"Stella, can I come and talk to you?"

Oh, this was strange. Not the fact that she wanted to talk to me, but that she sounded so *incredibly* near.

"Um. . . OK, when?"

"Well, now-ish. I think I'm quite close to your house but I got a bit lost. . ."

"Well, where do you think you are just now?"

"Um. . . I dunno. I'm in a scuzzy little lane,

164

and there's a big scary cat staring down at me."

Aha. Glancing over at Peaches, I saw him ogling something on the other side of the wall.

"Rachel, that's *my* cat. You met him a couple of days ago?" I said out loud, switching my phone off now that I realized we could hear each other's normal talking voices.

"Oh, yeah. . .!" I heard her girlie voice drift over from the alley.

Two minutes and some directions later, Rachel had come around to the front of our house and was now sitting with me in the den, a glass of orange juice in her hand. She hadn't touched the plate of biscuits that Mum had insisted we take out with us. (Think Mum was trying to help out during what looked like a "making up" meeting.)

"You w-w-w-want one?" I asked her, nerves getting the better of me as I held out the chocolate digestives.

"No, thanks," said Rachel, shaking her head so her hair half covered her face. I noticed she'd done a slightly different parting, so that the bruise on her cheek was covered by a shiny, dark brown curtain.

"Is your mum all right with you coming here on your own? In case you get sick again or something?"

I asked, the thought flickering through my head.

"She doesn't know I've come. But I just had to."

I hoped she would say whatever it was that she wanted to say quickly. I wasn't going to risk speaking again because I felt too edgy and worried in case all that came out was a garbled stammer.

"Prrrrr. . ." purred Peaches, tangling himself into a cat-shaped figure of eight around Rachel's skinny legs.

"Listen," she finally began, talking to me, but looking down at Peaches as she tried to gently extricate a foot without losing her balance and standing on him. "I was having a moan to my brother last night about what TJ called me."

Hmmm. I wasn't sure I wanted to hear the rest of what Rachel had to say now. If she *still* thought she was in the right, then I was the wrong person to be talking to.

"I told Si that TJ called me spoilt – and you know what he did?"

I shook my head, but she didn't see that, as she was bending down stroking Peaches now.

"He just laughed and said I *was*!"

As Rachel shrugged, I stayed schtum. I didn't know what to say, apart from that her brother had a point.

166

"Si said Mum and Dad let me get away with murder. Then he laughed some more and said me and Kayleigh and Hazel and Brooke were a gang of spoilt little rich girls!"

Oops. How funny. Not for Rachel though, I didn't suppose. . .

"I couldn't sleep last night for thinking about what Si said," Rachel mumbled. "Every time I closed my eyes, I kept seeing snatches of American movies with these horrible cliques of bitchy teen queens, and I thought, 'I don't *want* to be like that!'"

Oo-er.

The charitable thing might have been to say, "You're not *that* bad!", but I'd've been lying. 'Cause she certainly *could* be that bad, in her worst moments.

"Stella. . ." said Rachel, suddenly turning her head and staring up at me. "Have I been really horrible to you? Honestly?"

OK. Time for truth. Gulp.

"Yes, sometimes."

Actually, that felt quite good to get off my chest. Maybe I'd say a little more, specially since I'd managed that last bit without stammering.

"When you and Kayleigh and Brooke and Hazel were together, you were *really* horrible.

When I first arrived in Portbay, you lot used to look me up and down like I was trash."

"But I didn't *mean* it like that!" Rachel blurted out, straightening up now. "I thought you looked really interesting, and you had on all this really trendy stuff for round here!"

"Well, *Kayleigh* sure meant it when she asked me about my 'tan' at the lido. She said you were all talking about me."

Rachel's face was pinking up, and she had started nibbling the side of her mouth nervously.

"Oh, I guess that must have sounded kind of nasty. . ."

"Yes, it did," I replied bluntly.

"I'm . . . I'm sorry, Stella," Rachel mumbled, shamefaced. "It's just that Kayleigh always said you should be straight and just say stuff to people's faces."

"Even horrible stuff?"

Rachel blushed some more and couldn't quite look me in the eye.

"Some of the things that Kayleigh would come out with made me feel pretty bad, specially when she made me or Hazel or Brooke say them *for* her."

"Well, why did you do it, then?" I pushed.

"'Cause . . . 'cause I suppose I was always a bit

168

scared of her. I knew what she could be like and I thought she might turn on me."

"Which she did."

"Which she did." Rachel nodded slowly.

So. . . Kayleigh was more of the ringleader of the clique than I (and TJ) had ever thought. Mind you, Kayleigh wasn't the main person to ignore me and TJ the day after we did our rescue team bit.

"Y'know, you never said thank you to me and TJ for helping you at the lido," I pointed out.

Rachel pinked up even more.

"I was *so* embarrassed about what I must have looked like, I didn't want to be reminded of it, and you and TJ *really* reminded me of it! Plus, Kayleigh always said that none of us should get too friendly with other people, 'cause they'd want to muscle in on us."

Gee, Kayleigh sounded like a real fun character. I'd have to try saying her name to Peaches later and see what sort of reaction I got. He'd probably sick up furballs. . .

"Stella?" said Dad's voice suddenly, as he loomed at the doorway of the den. "TJ's on the house phone for you. You want to grab it?"

For half a second I thought about asking Dad to tell TJ I'd call him back later, but I really wanted to nip inside and quickly give him an update on what was happening. He'd probably just say, "She *apologized*? And you *really* believe she won't be horrible again? Ha ha ha ha. . .", but I still wanted to give it a try.

"Back in a minute," I told Rachel, leaving her bonding with Peaches.

"She apologized? And you really think she means it? Well, I don't get it, and I don't think that girl would be able to stay nice for more than half an hour at a time!"

Ah, well. Nearly guessed TJ's response right.

"Well, I think she's being genuine and. . . Uh-oh, here she comes!"

I dropped my voice to a whisper and then put my hand over the mouthpiece as I watched Rachel cross the garden and wander in through the kitchen door.

"Look, I've got to go," she said softly to me, like she didn't want to disturb my conversation. "But can we maybe meet up at the Shingle café tomorrow afternoon? Me, you and TJ? I'll buy you lunch, my treat. To say thank you for the lido . . . thing."

"Uh, OK," I answered with a shrug. "But aren't you worried about Kayleigh and Sam and that lot being in there?"

"Yeah, but I'm not going to let them bother me again. Not when I'm going to be sitting with my new friends!"

Yikes – she was kind of counting her chickens there. Maybe I'd be tempted to accept her apology, but I had a feeling TJ might be a teeny bit (make that a HUGE bit) reluctant.

"Right. . ." I said vaguely, waving her off. "See you there at one?"

"One o'clock – cool," said Rachel, heading towards the front door.

Five minutes after that, I was sitting at my desk in the den, wondering how I could persuade TJ to come tomorrow. When I'd mentioned it on the phone he'd absolutely insisted he wasn't going anywhere with "that rude cow".

As my head whirled, I idly put my hand in the drawer and tried to find the paper folder with the fake fairy photos in them. I could still be thinking things over as I scanned and sent them to the girls in London.

But my hand searched in vain. Had I taken them inside and left them somewhere? I didn't think so. Had the twins got their tricksy toddler hands on them and hidden them in the tumble dryer? No – the door to the den was always safely locked when I wasn't here.

Um – I knew this was going to sound insane, but had *Rachel* just helped herself to them?

OK, she might be all the things that TJ had called her, but I couldn't see her being a thief too. Er, could I. . .?

CHAPTER 17

U-turns of the brain. . .

SQUEET! Oink. SQUEET! Oink. SQUEET! Oink. SQUEET! Oink. . . .

Rachel really did seem to want to make up with us. Not only had she bought us lunch (pizza for TJ, tuna bake for me, double chocolate chocolate cake for us both), but she'd also brought along a pressie for Bob, which did a lot to heal the rift with TJ.

"He *loves* that thing!" TJ grinned out of the window, watching his dog lying on the pavement, happily chewing a pink rubber pig.

TJ had taken a lot of persuasion to come here today. I'd had to tell him about fourteen times that this was Rachel's one, last chance to be our friend.

"Yeah, but you say that *now*, Stella, then she'll go and be a pain *again*, and you'll go all girlie and forgive her *again*," TJ had grumbled on the phone yesterday.

"I promise I won't! She's so *totally* on probation – one false move and it's over!" I tried to reassure him.

But TJ still wouldn't agree to come along to the Shingles café. I finally had to resort to my last tactic of persuasion.

"I dare you."

"What?" he'd said.

"I dare you to come to lunch tomorrow. Or are you too chicken?"

Jake and Jamie had been pretty fascinated by my prancing hen impression and both boys had been clucking around the house every waking moment since, which was driving my dad a bit mad, actually.

Still, the dare worked, and got TJ here, even if he *had* turned up looking pretty grouchy. But as soon as Rachel presented Bob with her gift, you could see all the grouchiness slip-sliding away, to be replaced by TJ's natural state, i.e. easy-going, and at the moment, pretty hungry.

"That lot are doing my head in. Can they stare over and snigger any more?" muttered TJ, through his last mouthful of double chocolate chocolate cake.

The "they" were Sam and Kayleigh's newly

bonded crews, I knew *that* much without turning around to look.

"Ignore them. They're just hoping to get a response so they know they're bugging you."

"Wish *they'd* bug off," TJ growled, forcing himself not to glower back at them.

"Eat cake. Be happy," I told him, pushing Rachel's barely touched slab of chocolate cake in front of him.

"Didn't she want any more?" he asked.

"Nope. And she hardly ate her baked potato either. Hey, d'you think she's funny with food?"

"Like anorexic or something?" TJ said bluntly through his next mouthful of cake.

"Not anorexic or bulimic necessarily," I said hurriedly, hoping she wasn't in the loo right now chucking up what little she'd eaten. "It's just that she's so skinny, and I've never really seen her eating much of anything. She didn't touch that sundae Phil gave her the other day. And she didn't take a biscuit from me yesterday. . ."

I was about to launch into my theory – however far-fetched – that maybe not eating properly had helped make Rachel epileptic (I hadn't checked that on the web yet), when Amber the waitress wandered over with a tray and a scowl.

"This finished with?" she barked, pointing to the plates on the table.

"Mmm," I mumbled and nodded, a little bit scared of her. She could have only been a year or so older than me and TJ – fifteen at the most – but she acted like she was old enough to have the weight of the world on her hunched shoulders. Why did Phil the café owner employ her, I wondered? Her sour-puss face was enough to give his customers indigestion. . .

"Anyway, where *is* Rachel?" asked TJ, glancing in the direction of the loos, where Rachel had disappeared to ages ago. "She's not putting on a ton of make-up again, is she? That bruise has practically vanished!"

Instantly I decided to go check on her. Never mind make-up, or stupid notions of her barfing her lunch – what if she'd had a seizure in the loos, and was trapped behind the cubicle door? She could have hit her head and knocked herself out (the shame – knocking yourself unconscious on a toilet bowl. . .). Hadn't I read that *that* was the biggest danger? Hurting yourself when you fell during a seizure?

Quickly, I wended my way between the busy tables, heading for the loos and ignoring the several sets of eyes following me. I knew that

Rachel had specifically wanted to come here today to show Kayleigh and Sam and their horrible newly intertwined gangs that they couldn't upset her, but maybe she'd found it too hard to handle after all. What if the stress of that had made her feel ill?

Clattering through the door with the strange stick-like figure in a triangle that was supposed to be a skirt, the first thing I saw was a shut cubicle door (uh-oh!), and the first sound I heard was snivelling. (Hooray! If Rachel was crying, it meant she wasn't dead! Er, that sounds a bit heartless, but you know what I mean. . .)

"Rachel?" I said, tapping softly on the door. "What's up?"

"I – I can't tell you!"

"Why can't you tell me . . . whatever it is?" I asked, frowning like crazy but hoping the confusion wasn't too obvious in my voice.

"I'm too ashamed!"

"Um . . . well, if you can't tell me, why don't you try to forget about whatever it is for now, and just come out of there?" I suggested, without one single clue what was going on.

"I can't! I can't come out!"

"Huh? But you've got to come out *some*time! You can't stay there for ever!"

Suddenly the snivelling turned into wracking sobs. Honestly, this girl was the most confusing person I'd ever met. I'd never felt so angry and then so sorry for someone in such a short space of time. In the last week, Rachel had my brain doing so many U-turns I felt permanently dizzy. . .

"Rachel, *please*! Tell me what's wrong!" I said to the door. "Or do you want me to go along to the Galleria and get your mum for you?"

"*Noooo!*" she cried out. "I'd *die* of embarrassment!"

"Rachel, it can't be that bad!"

"But it is! 'Cause everyone will know I'm a liar and a freak!"

"Everyone *who*? What are you on about?"

"You and my mum and the doctors at the hospital . . . and if Kayleigh ever finds out, I'm dead!"

"What's Kayleigh got to do with it?!" I asked, even though I didn't know what "it" was. . .

But the only answer I got was a whole bunch of hiccuped sobs.

I didn't know what to do.

Rachel *had* to come out of there sometime this century, or at least tell me what was wrong. I thought fleetingly about trying to *dare* her to come out, but I couldn't see that working.

As far as I could figure out, there was only one thing I *could* do: blackmail her. It was harsh, but it was for her own good.

"Rachel, if you don't open this door and tell me what's going on now, I *am* going to go and get your mum!"

For a second there was silence, and then I heard a tiny *ftt!* sound. It was the sound of a bolt being drawn back. Before Rachel got a chance to change her mind, I barged in and shut the door behind me.

And there was Rachel, sitting on the lid of the loo seat, looking like the world had ended.

"Oh, Stella, you are going to think I'm a *complete* freak!"

Uh-oh.

What on earth was coming next? Was she going to admit to being a trainspotter or something? Or was she going to confess to being half-human, half-robot?

I dreaded to think. . .

CHAPTER 18

Fake fairies and flea spray

"What's going on?" asked TJ, staring at me as I sat down and began quickly rummaging through my bag. "Is Rachel OK?"

"TJ, I'm going to tell you something now," I said in a low, secretive voice. "And for this, I need you *not* to go all awkward and embarrassed. Actually, for this, I need you to pretend to be a girl for a minute. Can you pretend to be a girl?"

"What?!" TJ hissed back, looking horrified.

"Come on! Your parents are both actors – just try to act like you're a girl for *two* minutes while I let you in on something, OK?"

"Do I *have* to?"

"Yes!" I said with authority. "What I'm about to tell you is *dead* important, and I don't want any boy-ish 'urghs!' and 'yeeews!' out of you. Got it?"

TJ didn't *really* get it, but I think I alarmed him so much that he thought it was safest just to humour me.

180

And then I told him.

I told him that at the age of thirteen going on fourteen, Rachel had just started her first *ever* period.

This was a problem because over the course of their dubious friendship, Kayleigh Smith had drummed it into Rachel that if you didn't start your period by the time you were twelve, you were abnormal, which frightened the bejeezus out of Rachel so much that she pretended it had already happened for her. Kayleigh had done such a good job that Rachel even pretended the same thing to her mum.

And of course Rachel had even lied to the specialist at the hospital this last week. He'd mentioned that epilepsy in young women can happen around the same time that their periods start – 'cause of all the ping-ponging hormonal stuff going on – and instead of admitting that *that* might be what was happening to her, Rachel had found herself muttering that her periods had started *aeons* ago.

Now she was going to have to see him at the next appointment and tell him it had all been one stupid, time-wasting fib – which her mum was going to find out too.

The truth was, Rachel Riley's first ever period

started today, Sunday, at 1.55 p.m. And I was about to get her some emergency supplies from my bag.

"So what?" I'd said to her, as I passed her half a roll of toilet paper to blow her nose on. "The doctor and your mum are going to be so pleased that they've found a possible cause that they're not going to care! It's really no big deal! And it is *so* not weird to start your periods at thirteen – don't you read any teen mags?!"

Rachel had been a bit calmer by the end – not totally convinced calmer, but she was getting there. Calm enough for me to come out here and get my bag and fill TJ in, that was for sure.

"I see," nodded TJ slowly, when I'd finished. "That must be tough for her."

Aw, bless him – TJ was doing an excellent job of listening like a girl, to a girls-only story. Not once had he "urgh"ed, "yewww"ed or pulled a face. Yes, he had a glint of uncomfortable panic in his eyes, but I had to give him ten out of ten for his efforts.

"Back in a minute. . ." I told him, heading back towards the loo.

Poor Rachel, I thought, as I leant on the cool, white sink and waited for her to sort herself out. She'd always tried to come across so confident and cocky, but all the time she was clueless and scared about something boringly normal in a girl's life. And there was me being ignorant, wondering if her not eating had anything to do with her epilepsy.

"You know, I thought you were skinny 'cause you didn't eat," I told her through the door, realizing that the lack of periods was the reason she didn't have much in the way of boobs or hips.

"Huh? But I *do* eat!"

"You never ate much of your lunch. And you never ate that free sundae Phil gave you. . ."

"Yeah, but the baked potato was all hard and horrible today. And I don't really like sweet things – I just got the chocolate cake 'cause you guys were having it. I like crisps and stuff better!"

As she chattered and sounded more relaxed, the lock on the cubicle door went *ftt!* again and Rachel emerged.

"OK?" I smiled at her.

"Yeah . . . yeah, I'm OK," she smiled shyly.

"Let's get out of here then, and we'll go for a walk along to Sugar Bay or something," I suggested, holding the door open for Rachel.

"Yes, I'd like tha—"

"LADIES AND GENTLEMEN! WILL YOU PLEASE WELCOME RACHEL RILEY, DOING

HER AMAZING RENDITION OF KYLIE'S 'CAN'T GET YOU OUT OF MY HEAD'! GIVE IT UP FOR RACHEL."

"Stella?" whimpered Rachel, hovering one foot in the air as she tried to leave the sanctuary of the ladies' loos. "What's Phil doing? I can't sing! What if I have another seizure?!"

"COME ON, LADIES AND GENTLEMEN! THE GIRL NEEDS A LITTLE ENCOURAGE-MENT!" Phil boomed into the karaoke mike. "WHAT ABOUT A DYNAMITE ROUND OF APPLAUSE AND SOME WHOOPING PLEASE!"

I wasn't sure what to do. I already knew that Rachel had a great singing voice – what I *couldn't* do was reassure her she wouldn't have another seizure. But maybe if I could get her to concentrate on *something* positive, it would stop her from fretting and making herself ill *that* way.

"That 'sense' thing you've been feeling . . . d'you think you could try and concentrate on that? Can you maybe feel how this is going to go, and how you'll be feeling in five minutes, once you've done your song?"

Phil had done a good job on the customers this Sunday afternoon – the clapping and cheering was almost overwhelming. For a long second,

Rachel looked scared, then she did that strange blank thing for a moment, as if she really could sense what might be in store.

"OK, I'll do it. . ." she murmured to me, walking over and taking the microphone from a beaming Phil.

As Rachel began belting out a brilliant version of Kylie's old hit song, I slipped into my seat next to TJ.

"She looks good, doesn't she?" I said, moving my chair round to see Rachel better and nudging TJ with my elbow.

"I guess so – if you like skinny, big-headed, moody girls," said TJ with a grin, sounding and looking his normal, boy-ish self once again.

"Hopefully this'll help her get her confidence back a bit," I murmured, ignoring TJ's teasing. "Lucky that Phil suddenly came up with the idea of her doing a turn again just now!"

"Er . . . not so much luck, actually," TJ said with a shrug.

"What d'you mean?" I frowned at him, while the whole of the café (with the possible exception of new queen bee Kayleigh Smith and her cronies) clapped along with Rachel.

"I asked Phil to do it," said TJ matter-of-factly, "while you guys were in the loo. I thought it was like that old getting-straight-back-on-to-the-bicycle-when-you've-fallen-off thing again."

TJ – he really wasn't your average boy, either in height or thoughtfulness (what he lacked in the first, he more than made up for in the second).

"Y'know, she was worried she'd feel another attack coming on," I told him, not taking my eyes off Rachel as she sang. "I tried to get her to think like she was psychic before she went up there, just to give her a lift. And she did that whole blank, staring thing, as if she really could sense something!"

"What sort of something?" TJ asked. "Like something happening to Kayleigh and Sam and the others?"

I thought that was a pretty weird/dumb thing to say – till I heard a few overlapping coughs start to happen. Suddenly, there were more coughs (and a couple of swear words), all coming from the table where Kayleigh, Sam and the others were sitting.

People around the café were turning and scowling at them, shushing them grumpily as Rachel closed her almond eyes and reached effortlessly for the high notes.

"What's going on with them?" I wondered aloud to TJ.

And how on earth had he known that something was *about* to happen to them? Was he turning psychic on me too, same as Rachel?

But Rachel's moment of glory was over, ending this time – thankfully – to cheers and applause instead of trembling and ambulances. . .

"You did brilliantly!" I beamed at her, as she flopped happily down beside us, clapping still ringing in all our ears.

"It was OK, 'cause like you said, I tried to concentrate and tune in to what might happen."

"And did you 'sense' everyone cheering for you like this?" I grinned at her.

"No," she said with a giggle. "I know this is going to sound totally weird, but I just felt really, really sure that something was going to happen to Kayleigh and the others. I didn't know what it would be; all I knew was that it would stop them hassling me and I could get on with what I was doing!"

"Wow. . ." I muttered, stunned, as I glanced over at the back table where several people from Kayleigh and Sam's crew were missing, and whoever was still there was coughing or madly gulping down glasses of water or juice or whatever. "You really are kind of psychic, aren't you, Rach?"

"Well, *I'm* not psychic, and *I* knew that was going to happen," smiled TJ.

"How?" I frowned at him. Again. (This was becoming a habit.)

"'Cause I asked Amber the waitress for a favour. . ." he said enigmatically.

"TJ, you'd *better* explain more, or I'm going to ping sugar cubes at your head till they leave dents," I warned him.

"Well, I gave Amber a couple of quid and asked her to give Kayleigh and that lot a plate of cheesy nachos 'on the house'. Only with extra, *extra* helpings of chilli. . ."

I remembered the one time I'd accidentally bitten on a hunk of green chilli pepper on a pizza and felt like I needed to suck on a tap for twenty-four hours just to put out the fire in my head and mouth. That must be *exactly* what was happening to "lovely" Kayleigh and co right now.

TJ – how smart was he? (And how long had he been looking for any small, sweet revenge on all those guys?)

"Amber helped? But how come? She doesn't look like the kind that would put herself out to do a favour," I said, watching the round-shouldered girl scoop empty mugs off a nearby table with all the enthusiasm of an undertaker.

"Amber's all right," shrugged TJ, eating his last forkful of double chocolate chocolate cake.

"Hey, Rach," I turned and smiled at her. "Why don't you just wave to all your fans and we'll get out of here?"

"Brilliant idea," Rachel nodded, looking a hundred times sparkier than she had only five or so minutes ago. I suddenly felt so proud of me and TJ – I'd done an excellent job of sorting out the girlie stuff Rachel had got herself in a tizz about, and TJ had done an amazing job of wreaking a little revenge (for all of us, let's face it) and bolstering Rachel's soggy confidence into the bargain.

I only hoped that this once – *finally* – Rachel would realize that *we* were the good guys.

"C'mon, I've got something to show you two. . ." Rachel muttered, while leaving cash for lunch on the table and waving at her holidaymaking fans.

"Oh, yeah?" said TJ, trying to coax a happily entertained Bob along the pavement of the prom. "What's that, then, Rach?"

SQUEET! Oink. SQUEET! Oink. SQUEET! Oink . . . squeaked Bob's new toy as he reluctantly followed the three of us.

"Not telling," smiled Rachel, walking along the length of shops (past Madame Xara's place AND Madame Xara's cheese palace. . .).

"What's the big mystery?" I asked, pleased to see her looking so happy after looking so bottom-dropped-out-of-her-world miserable not so long ago.

"There!" she smiled in triumph, pointing to the window of the Portbay Galleria, i.e. her mum's posh arty-crafty shop.

"There *what*?" I frowned, glancing quickly at the usual assortment of dull seascapes and ornaments of mystery objects made out of shells.

And then I saw them.

At the same time TJ saw them.

Two of our Fake Fairy Photo Project snaps, blown up large and mounted in classy, dark brown frames.

"But what are they doing here?" I asked vaguely, marvelling at how gorgeous our pictures looked, but still having room to stress over the fact that these were stolen – out of my desk in the den yesterday morning. . .

"Don't flip out on me for taking these, Stella!" Rachel begged. "I just thought they were brilliant the first time I saw them in the café, and I wanted to do something nice for you two as a surprise,

190

just to say thanks for looking out for me and everything."

"They look great," I said, turning my attention back to the framed pictures in the window. "And your mum was cool about you putting them in her window?"

"*Better* than that – my mum *loves* them! *And* she's going to put them in the art show for the Portbay Gala next week. And she said that already this morning she had people coming in and asking to buy them, but she wanted me to bring you along here today to check that you were OK with that before she started to get more prints made up to sell them!"

They'd be put on show in an exhibition? And we might make some money out of them? That had never happened to those original fake fairy schoolgirls. . .

Maybe there'd be enough money from the sale of these to pay for all my old friends from London to come down and visit me at the same time. The house was too grotty and dilapidated for them to stay in, so we could all go to a hotel and order room-service pizza all night! (With *no* chillis. . .)

Or maybe I'd have enough dosh to hire a private detective to try and find my long-lost grandad Eddie (and maybe Rachel could give me a few spooksome, psychic clues to help get him started?).

"Hey, Bob, maybe with *my* share, we could get you a can of flea spray, eh?" TJ said to his happily scratching dog, who looked back up at him with his new pig toy in his jaws, probably hoping that his master had just said, "Blah blah blah lots of sausages blah."

"*Flea* spray!" snorted Rachel, looking down at Bob and cringing. "What are you *like*, Beanie B –"

Catching the same "don't-you-dare!" looks on me and TJ's faces, Rachel immediately reined herself in.

"Was I doing it again?" she asked, blinking her pretty almond eyes at us. "I'm sorry, I really *will* try harder. . ."

Rachel Riley: she was a bit spoilt; she'd been high and mighty (and mean), thanks to the influence of Kayleigh Smith; and her moods had wobbled all over the place 'cause she was scared about what was happening to her (the epilepsy), what *hadn't* happened to her (her periods) and anyone finding out the truth (like it was any big deal).

But underneath the weirdness and the spoilt brat act and the selfishness, there were enough glimpses of a decent girl for me and TJ to give her a chance.

What would me and TJ teach her? Well, how to be nice, and how to have *fun* – without it being at other people's expense.

And any time Rachel slipped back into her old, mean, teen queen ways; well, we'd just have to feed Bob the smelliest tin of dog food, then order him to go lick Rachel's perfect(ly horrified) face, wouldn't we. . .?

From: Frankie
To: *stella*
Subject: Stella Stansfield, super-hero!

Hi, Stella the super-hero!!

Saved any more lives recently? Grabbed any babies out of burning buildings or pushed grannies out of the path of hurtling, runaway double decker buses?

Ha! Sorry, I know it bugs you when I'm in teasing mode, but hey, that's just me, so live with it or ship out. (Oh, you did already! All the way to Portbay. . .)

Anyway, glad to hear that little Miss Attitude Rachel seems OK-ish now, specially since she's not hanging out with those drongo mates of hers any more. And you know, the more I hear about him, the more I'm warming to TJ – the extra, *extra* hot chilli peppers in the nachos was an excellent idea! I'm going to Pizza Hut with the girls tonight. I might save a few chillis to put on Eleni's plate when she's not looking – she's still being seriously funny with me about how much time I spend with Seb.

Only joking – I wouldn't really do that to her (I think!).

194

Gotta go meet them – I'll say hi and hugs from you.
Miss you ☹, but M8s 4eva ☺!
Frankie

PS I think you might be on to something when you said Peaches could be a small alien in a cat-suit. *Definitely* look for hidden buttons under his armpits. . .

PPS Write back and tell me more about that tourist girl you've been hanging out with. What's her name again? Megan or something? And what exactly did her nutty sister do. . .? You know I love a great big dollop of gossip – more soon, please!

Coming soon...

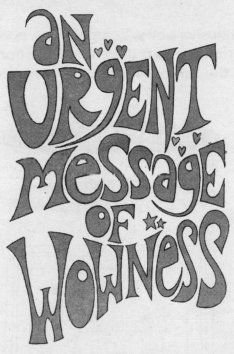

AN URGENT MESSAGE OF WOWNESS

Heather thinks everyone in her family comes from Planet Perfect. Everyone except her, that is. Then Dad drops a bombshell, and the world turns upside down...

Life's become surprising, exciting and just a little bit mad – but is this topsy-turvy new family somewhere Heather can fit in?

A scrumptious new novel from best-selling author
Karen McCombie.

SIGN UP NOW!

For exclusive news, competitions and further information about Karen and her books, sign up to the Karen McCombie newsletter now!

Just email

publicity@scholastic.co.uk

And don't forget to check out her website –

www.karenmccombie.com

Karen says...

"It's sheeny and shiny, furry and er, funny in places! It's everything you could want from a website and a weeny bit more..."

KAREN McCOMBIE

Once upon a time (OK., 1990), Karen McCombie jumped in her beat-up car with her boyfriend and a very bad-tempered cat, leaving her native Scotland behind for the bright lights of London and a desk at "J17" magazine. She's lived in London and acted like a teenager ever since.

The fiction bug bit after writing short stories for "Sugar" magazine. Next came a flurry of teen novels, and of course the best-selling "Ally's World" series, set around and named after Alexandra Palace in North London, close to where Karen lives with her husband Tom, little daughter Milly and an assortment of cats.

To: You
From: Stella
Subject: Stuff

Hi,

You'd think it would be cool to live by the sea with all that sun, sand and ice cream. But, believe me, it's not such a breeze. I miss my best mate Frankie, my terror twin brothers drive me nuts and my mum and dad have gone daft over the country dump, sorry, "character cottage", that we're living in. I'm bored, and I'm fed up with being the new girl on the block.
Hey! Maybe if we hang out together we could have some fun here. Whadya think?
Catch up with me in the rest of the *Stella Etc.* series.
I bet we'll have loads to talk about.
CU soon.
LOL

stella
XXX

PS Here's a pic of me on a bad hair day (any day actually) with my mate Frankie. I'm the one on the right!

"Super-sweet and cool as an ice cream" *Mizz*

Stella Etc. – 7 titles in paperback at £4.99
from all good bookshops